Tell Me

By Ashe Barker

Copyright © 2016 by Ashe Barker Books.
All rights reserved.

This book or any portion thereof may not be reproduced or used in any manner whatsoever without the express written permission of the author except for the use of brief quotations in a book review. This book is intended for adults only. Spanking and other sexual activities represented in this book are a work of fiction, intended for adults. This book is a work of fiction. Names, characters, places, and incidents are used fictitiously by the author. Any resemblance to actual places, events, or persons, living or dead, is entirely coincidental.

Tell me, Thea.

After months of frequenting her local BDSM club, Thea has found what every submissive dreams of, the perfect Dom. He understands every gasp and shiver of her response and gives her exactly what she craves. He pushes her limits, takes her to the edge and then holds her while she floats back to reality. He knows every inch of her body in intimate detail, but nothing else about her at all. Though he tries to delve into her personal life, he respects her wishes when she refuses. Thea feels compelled to keep her 'real' life separate from anything that happens on the BDSM scene, it's the only way she can exist.

Tony is bewitched from the first moment he lays eyes on his perfect little sub at The Wicked Club. Months of scening with her only makes him crave more. But any pressure for information about her private life has her scurrying away like a frightened kitten. He needs to keep his cool and take it slow in order not to scare her away.

That is until a twist of fate lands Thea in Mr Tony diMarco's office and her worlds collide. Her perfect Dom is sitting behind the desk at her new job. It's too much and she refuses to mix her personal and professional lives. But Tony won't take no for an answer. He needs Thea Richmond in his bed and in his office and he is determined to have his way.

Thea is reluctant to blur the lines, but it's becoming more and more difficult to maintain her well-ordered existence. Will she trust her Dom to push her to the edge like he always does? Or will she risk losing the man she has come to love?

Chapter one

"Sir, stop... Please, I can't..." Thea allowed her head to drop backwards, dislodging the loose knot her Dom had fashioned in her hair at the start of their scene. It tumbled down her back in dark waves, a light caress against her shoulders, tender from the lash of the flogger. She hissed in a sharp breath, battling to ride the waves of exquisite agony shooting in a direct line from her clamped nipples to her clit.

The relentless flogging paused. Thea gasped, dragging in precious oxygen during this brief lull. A few seconds, just a few sweet moments would be enough for her to regroup and be ready to continue.

"Sir stop? Since when was that a safe word, girl?" Thea's pussy clenched at the low, rich tone of the man behind her, as he leaned forward now to murmur the words right into her ear. He had a unique quality in his voice, some special timbre which seemed to resonate right through her soul. She could never say no to him.

"It isn't. I mean, I don't want to stop, I apologise, Sir."

"Tell me, Thea." He reached around her to cup her breasts in his hands, briefly relieving the tension created by the nipple clamps gripping each of her swollen nubs. Thea sighed in relief, loving the intimacy of this moment, the certainty that he knew, without her even needing to tell him, that she was close to her limit.

Except she *had* told him. She *had* asked him to stop, though not in the customary manner, the manner guaranteed to bring a scene to a shuddering halt. If she'd uttered her safe word her Dom would have released her from the restraints which held her suspended from the beam across the ceiling in the dungeon. There would be no questions asked, she would be whisked straight into the aftercare suite. There she would be wrapped in a blanket and snuggled up to his warm solid body before she could say ball gag.

Thea hadn't said 'red'; but through her tone, her body language, he knew anyway.

Tony always knew.

"I just need a moment, Sir. Oh, that feels good." Thea allowed her head to rest against her Dom's shoulder as he massaged her breasts, his fingers gentle against her delicate, sensitive skin. For several more seconds he caressed her, drawing her back into the scene, back under his spell. He seemed to know the exact moment she was his again.

"We continue?"

"Yes, Sir. Please,"

There was a faint swirl of air against her naked back as he stepped away, and a rustle as he bent to retrieve the flogger he had laid to one side in order to calm her.

Thea shivered, then exhaled as he drew the strands of the flogger across her shoulders, her already heated skin prickling under the caress. He walked around her to trail the suede tendrils over her breasts, paying close attention to her throbbing nipples. Thea tensed, willing him not to flick or nudge, but at the same time longing for him to do just that.

He didn't. Instead he brushed her lips with his own, just the lightest suggestion of a kiss before he circled around behind her again. Thea wondered if it was possible to die from longing, from sheer anticipation.

"Sir…"

"I know." His tone was clipped, all business. Gone now the tender lover of just a few seconds ago, "Now, right?"

"Now, Sir … aaagh" Despite her readiness Thea let out a startled yelp as the flogger landed across her naked shoulders. The pain was sharp at first, shimmering across the surface of her skin, then sinking into her flesh, rich and heavy. She sagged forward, allowing the restraints which held her secure by the wrists to take her weight now.

Wordless, her Dom continued to drop stroke after stroke across her shoulders and buttocks, her breasts, her hips, each one perfectly placed and timed to ensure she had sufficient space to absorb the impact before the next fell. His movements were economical, efficient, precise, his skill long-practised. He circled her slowly, her body open to him, exposed.

Thea had been unnerved at first when Tony led her to the centre of the dungeon and asked her to raise her arms above her head. She had expected to be secured to the St Andrew's cross, which would have offered a modicum of privacy as she could have pressed her body against its warm, solid arms. Instead she was here, on display for the entire dungeon to watch as Tony worked his magic on her. Once he had her secured he had taken his time removing the corset which she had laced so carefully before leaving her flat. It now lay beside his bag of toys, a brilliant, shimmering pool of crimson. She was next to naked, but her self-consciousness had evaporated quickly, as they both knew it would.

The pinch of nipple clamps, the caress of the collar around her neck, these grounded her, gave her the solid foundation she craved. And Tony's voice, like liquid lust poured into her soul, just swept her along and carried her with him on this journey.

Thea counted the strokes in her head, picking up where they had left off before she begged for a time out, fifteen, sixteen, seventeen. She had enough experience now to recognise the moment her endorphins kicked in to blunt the intensity, to welcome that heady rush that felt like flying but through treacle. She was straining, reaching, almost, not quite…

"Enough." The sweet whipping stopped, and Tony stepped back in front of her. His expression was stern. She cringed, but still couldn't stem the words of protest.

"No, not yet. I need more. Sir, please." Thea shivered, her pussy clenching, her clit swollen and throbbing. *So close, so fucking close.* Gentle, firm hands unfastened the buckles securing her wrists. Thea slumped forward to be caught in Tony's arms. He hauled her against him, holding her for the few moments it took for her legs to regain enough sensation to support her.

"You stopped too early, I was almost there."

Her petulant tone was not to his liking if the sharp slap to her bottom was any indication. "I decide when you've had enough, not you. I've warned you enough times about topping from the bottom."

Thea was contrite instantly. "I'm sorry, I didn't mean to. You know best, I realise that. Thank you Sir." Despite her desire for more, Thea had no wish to earn a punishment, not in her current delicate, fragile state. She was physically close to her limit, and emotionally strung out to the point where she couldn't think straight. His anger now would be unbearable. She hesitated for a few moments, waiting for his response. Was he displeased?

It would seem not. His arms remained around her body, offering support, comfort, security.

Relieved and reassured Thea attempted to stand upright, damping down the bitter frustration of unmet need, unsatisfied lust. Tony pulled her back against him, turning her now so her shoulders rested against his chest. He cupped her breasts in his hands. Thea gasped, the forgotten nipple clamps now back in sharp focus. Tony chuckled as he pressed his palms against the pebbled nubs, pinched mercilessly in the clover-leaf grips.

"Not done yet, my sweet slut. I think we need something a little more—severe—to satisfy you this evening. Would you agree?"

Thea nodded, her yearning almost palpable, like a living, breathing entity snapping around her ankles, demanding satisfaction.

"The bench. Lay across it." He turned her in the direction of a spanking bench a few yards away in another part of the dungeon. Thea was oblivious to the presence of other couples engaged in similar play to her own, and to her own near-nakedness as she walked slowly over the warm, polished wood floor. She wore only her thong, as a passing nod to The Wicked Club's rule forbidding nudity in public areas, and the studded leather collar which Tony insisted on locking around her neck at the start of every scene they played.

Her body was sore, delightfully so, every movement reminding her of what she was, what she craved and why she was here. She reached the bench and draped her body across it, knowing exactly the right position to gain maximum exposure to whatever Tony would offer her next.

She turned her head to see her Dom crouch beside his bag, the rucksack he always used to carry his toys and equipment. He rarely played with anything other than his own personal items, things he knew, and could use with consummate skill. He selected his next implement.

The cane.

A ripple of terrified anticipation spiked through Thea's nervous system, causing her to jerk on the bench. Tony caught the movement and turned to regard her, his expression stony.
"Will you need me to tie you in place?"
"No, Sir." Thea bristled a little at the suggestion. She was no newbie, she knew what a caning was like, and she loved the bite of the rattan against the backs of her thighs. Maybe not while it was actually happening, but always afterwards. Without fail.
Tony straightened and leaned on the bench beside her. Thea had to twist her neck to keep him in sight.
"Are you sure? You know I won't permit you to move once we start. I have no wish to punish you this evening if that can be avoided so if you think you may fail in this I'm prepared to help you."
"I'll be fine, Sir. I promise."
"Good girl." The cane in his left hand, Tony caressed her waiting buttocks with his right palm, pressing on the areas she knew must be already crimson from the flogging. "How many strokes do you want?"
"You decide, Sir. You know how it needs to be." Which was code for *You know how much I need.*
"Okay, until I decide to stop then." He stood and moved into position behind her.
Thea nodded, then realised he could no longer see her head so she verbalised her agreement. He wouldn't start otherwise.
"Yes, Sir."
Her active participation now concluded, Thea allowed her slim frame to drape over the bench with a fluid, boneless grace. Her head felt heavy, her thinking slurred already as she sank deeper into her submissive haze.
She let out a sharp hiss as the first stroke landed across both cheeks of her arse.
"Wake up, subbie. Do I have your attention?" Tony sounded impatient, his words clipped and curt. Her head cleared in an instant.
"Yes, Sir. Sorry."
"Good. We can continue then." Tony shifted his position slightly to stand at right angles to her upturned bum. From her position across

the bench Thea could pick out the sharp crease of his smart trousers and the shine of his gleaming leather shoes, but he was obscured from the knees up.

He almost always met her in the club foyer, dressed for business, and she assumed he came to the club straight from work. She had no idea what her Dom did for a living, had never asked as that would involve trading confidences and she had no wish to discuss her own life beyond the confines of The Wicked Club.

She was different in the outside world, separate, another person entirely.

Thea held her breath as Tony tapped the cane against her bottom, the right cheek this time. He delivered a series of light, rapid taps then pressed the cane hard against her sensitised buttock. He waited for a couple of seconds, then lifted the cane and brought it down with a sharp snap in the exact place he had prepared.

Thea sighed, her clit quivering in near orgasm. The pain was wonderful, utterly sublime. A punishment caning would feel different. There would be no lead-in, no preparing her, no brief interlude between each stroke to allow the bite to sink deep into her tissues. Punishment was hard, relentless, cruel, whereas this was exquisite. She'd been on the receiving end of harsh discipline, also at Tony's hands, and knew the difference. Here, now, her Dom was intent on bringing her to the state of relaxed liberation she craved.

She had been right earlier, he knew exactly how it needed to be. How *she* needed to be.

Tony shifted again and repeated the sequence on her left buttock. This time the final stroke felt harder, more intense. Thea screamed. Tony ignored her and started his preparations on the next spot he'd selected. Back to her right buttock now, but an inch or so lower than the first time. Thea groaned as he pressed the cane into her flesh, lifting her bottom to welcome the final slicing blow.

"Oh God. Sir, that's so good. I want to come."

"Really?" Tony slid his hand between her legs and nudged the brief film of the thong to one side. He slid two fingers deep into her pussy, then withdrew them to inspect the wetness he had collected. "I believe you may be right. But that would be such a bad idea, little slut. You know the rules about orgasms without permission."

"I know, but I need to come, Sir. I need you to rub my clit."

"Like this?" He flicked the tip of her swollen bud with the pad of his finger, then drew it slowly across the end. Thea stiffened, thrusting her bottom up, her legs spread wide. It was to no avail, Tony withdrew his hand after just a couple of seconds. "I don't think so, not quite yet. We haven't finished here,"

"Oh, Sir, please."

"Hush. Concentrate." He started the ritual tapping again, this time on the spot at the back of her right thigh where it would hurt like hell tomorrow, and the day after, every time she sat down. The final stripe was like liquid fire, seeping into her bones. Thea was sobbing now, an emotional response to the extreme arousal, the intimacy, the humiliation, her absolute submission to the Dom who owned her for this night.

Another stroke to her left thigh had Thea squirming against the bench, her fingers gripping the solid wood legs of it as she fought the urge to reach back and cover her abused bottom, to beg him to stop.

She knew he was ramping this up, even the rapid taps against her skin were hurting as he prepared for the next stroke, on her bottom again this time. She let out another scream as the cane landed for the big one.

Tony paused, allowed her time to get her breath back. He would stop if she asked him, or even if she just gave him a signal she'd had enough. She wouldn't, not yet, or at least not intentionally. So often Tony just knew when to stop, as he had earlier. But she wanted more. She was hurting but she craved the pain. She needed to feel that final surge of energy, that rush of endorphin-fuelled lust that would drive her past the point of no return.

She'd experienced it before, many times. The sensation reminded her of a cork popping. Then, the pressure valve opened, whatever it was that screwed her up and messed with her head would flow out, freely. She would be rid of the tension, the pent up anxieties that plagued her, built up day after day, week after week and ground her down.

Tony would know. The moment she was free, he would know.

Thea reached for it, trusting Tony to take her to that place.

The next stroke was to be in the exact same spot he'd just caned. Tony started tapping, the mini-strokes falling so fast she couldn't tell one from another. Thea inhaled, the action automatic, ingrained, then she held the breath as he pressed the cane against her smarting bottom. Even so, despite her relaxed, near-euphoric state, the final stroke was excruciating. Thea screamed, then shuddered violently as her muscles tensed. The action was involuntary, sending aftershocks of sensation through her. Tony moved in close, slipped his hand between her legs again and this time his caress was long and purposeful. He massaged her clit, at the same time sliding two fingers inside her to curl against her G-spot. She groaned, squeezing, loving his touch, needing him to stay this time. Tony seemed to read her mind. He knew, as ever, the precise moment to flick the switch, to turn pain into pleasure, the contrast between the two heightening both. Or perhaps they were near-identical, perhaps that was why she couldn't seem to find one without the other.

"Now."

One word, enough. Her orgasm washed through her, the waves of pleasure pulsing, spinning her head around, scrambling what was left of conscious thought. The first release was powerful, therapeutic, cleansing. It was followed by a series of smaller after-tremors—less intense but equally satisfying—filling her cold, rigid frame with warmth, light, a sense of well-being.

Thea had no idea how long she lay there, Tony's hands on her, in her, drawing out her demons and replacing them with the quiet glow of submission, of safety, of peace.

The shudders had left her body, and she was only dimly aware of his fingers stroking her breasts as he released the clamps on her nipples, then the brisk rubbing of his palms on the sensitive nubs to dissipate the sharp pain as the blood rushed back. All the time his soft voice seemed to surround her, his words muffled but offering encouragement, approval, admiration.

She mewled a little as a soft blanket fell over her tender shoulders and back. His hands under her body raised her from the bench, turned her, then lifted her. She relaxed into Tony's arms as he murmured words into her ear, words she hardly registered as she snuggled into him.

Tony set her down on a sofa in the aftercare lounge, then settled beside her. Thea crawled into his arms, the blanket still wrapped around her as she began to shiver. Tony pulled it tighter, tucking in the edges.

"Do you need another blanket? A warm drink?"

She nodded, grateful for his close attention. "Tea please, in a minute."

She was vaguely aware of Tony summoning one of the wait staff and ordering a pot of tea, glad he could manage to do so without relaxing his embrace. She needed this now, this closeness. She desired Tony's gentle, warm brand of aftercare as much as she had craved his dominance earlier. He was an expert with a whip, a flogger, or a cane, but he came into his own with the cuddles afterwards. It was one of the reasons she adored scening with him, one of the reasons she could contemplate no other Dom since they had started to play together.

She curled up in his lap, his arms around her. Thea laid her cheek on his chest, loving the feel of the expensive silk mix of his shirt, cool against her face. He smoothed the hair back from her forehead and dropped a light kiss on the top of her head.

"I'll be alright soon. Just a few minutes…"

"No rush, sweetheart. We have all night. Or I do."

"I need to get home."

"Yeah? Why's that then?"

"I, I just do. But you haven't… I mean, would you like to find a private room?"

"You beg me to fuck you most times, and it's no hardship to oblige. But it's not mandatory. You're tired, pretty wrung out in fact, and as a rule I prefer my subs to be conscious when I fuck them. I think we're done here. Apart from this, of course." He tightened his arms around her, hauling her up against him and rubbing large circles on her back. "Ah, here's your tea."

"I love this… with you. Sir." Thea's words were a soft whisper, barely audible. Despite her submissive nature she often struggled to admit out loud to feeling vulnerable. And gratitude was way up there on the same scale of personal risk-taking as far as she was concerned. It was a measure of her trust in Tony that she could say as much as she had.

"You earn it. Every time, but that was an intense scene. More than usual. Is there anything wrong?"

"Wrong? What do you mean? I thought you said I did well…"

"That's not what I mean. You were very—needy. Demanding, as though you had demons to exorcise. So I wondered what caused that."

"Nothing. At least, nothing here. With you."

"Okay, I get that you're entitled to your privacy and I'm not prying. But we are friends, yes? You know you can talk to me. I can listen almost as well as I can handle a flogger."

"I do know. It's not that, and not you. I just, I like to keep things separate. It's better that way."

"I'm not sure I agree, but if you insist. You have my mobile number. Use it if you change your mind. Shall I pour?"

Thea nodded, and considered the matter closed. She wriggled into a sitting position but despite her reluctance to open up to him, and her claims that she had to get home, she was in no real hurry to separate from Tony's comforting warmth. She took the offered cup of steaming tea and sipped slowly, allowing her body time to drift gently back down from the endorphin-induced high. She spotted a couple of chocolate biscuits on the tray beside the teapot and nibbled one of those. Her blood sugar needed a boost.

How long had she been scening with Tony now? Six months? Eight, perhaps. They met here at the club every couple of weeks or so, and to Thea's way of thinking each scene was more intense than the last. More satisfying. More fulfilling. As the days passed between their encounters she would long for her Dom's summons. Eventually he would text her, usually a curt few words and giving her just hours' notice. Today had been no exception

Tonight. Nine thirty. Corset. High heels.

Her response… *Yes, Sir.*

She let her mind drift back to the evening she met this tall, dark haired Dom. She had been coming to The Wicked Club alone for a couple of months, watching other members enjoying the facilities, attending demonstrations of wax play or bondage techniques. She enjoyed regular spankings administered by the dungeon staff when she requested it, and those were quite delightful. She was happy, blending in and anonymous in her kink. She certainly wasn't looking for a regular Dom.

In fairness, Tony was no regular Dom. He was simply—perfect. From the first moment he strolled up to her, flashed that ebony-eyed smile and invited her to join him for a drink she was under his spell. He was attractive, but Thea thought that was true of all Doms. They exuded a certain—something—that drew her in. With Tony it was more. His classic good looks were just part of it. He looked to be a little older than she was, perhaps in his mid-thirties, and smartly dressed. Thea loved a man in a well-tailored suit and Tony was the epitome of male elegance. His dark grey jacket and trousers were immaculate, his crisp white shirt pristine. He removed his burgundy and grey striped tie as they sat in the bar and unbuttoned his collar. Thea thought she might dissolve into a puddle at his feet.

Tony's physical perfection was just a part of his appeal though. He was unfailingly courteous, he smiled a lot, and when he invited her to accompany him back into the dungeon she was more than happy to drape herself over a spanking bench for him. He had never disappointed her, delivering just the right level of intensity to satisfy her craving for pain. Submissive to her core, Thea rarely attracted anything approaching discipline from her Dom, but on the rare occasions he did harden his tone with her or raise a disapproving eyebrow her pussy melted. She just quivered, her desire for his dominance bringing her to her knees every time.

She had scened with no one else since that first time with Tony. She had no desire to. He had set the standard as far as she was concerned and no other Dom would measure up. He had set the bar high, yet she didn't even know his last name. She had no wish to know. Tony was her guilty secret, he existed here at The Wicked Club. In this place, with this powerful Dom, she could let herself go, safe in the knowledge that the Thea who stripped in public and orgasmed on a growled command, was a world away from the prim, efficient woman who inhabited her everyday life. And never the twain should meet.

"Sweetheart, are you falling asleep?"

"What? Oh, sorry…" Thea's musings came to an abrupt end, disturbed by her Dom's soft voice. His aftercare was intoxicating, but Thea knew she could postpone the inevitable no longer. "I need to be off."

"Do you have a taxi booked?"

"No, I wasn't sure how long we'd be."

"I'll call one, while you get dressed. Unless you want me to drop you off?" He raised one eyebrow, his expression mischievous. They both knew she absolutely refused to accept a lift home. Ever. It was better that no one at The Wicked Club knew where she lived, even Tony. He often offered, and she always turned him down.

Ten minutes later, decently dressed in her long overcoat, which completely covered her fetish outfit beneath, Thea scrambled into a taxi at the foot of the entrance steps in front of the club. She lifted a hand to Tony, his smile and sexy wink as the vehicle pulled away causing her pussy to clench despite the bone-deep satisfaction he'd already provided.

Tony always did have that effect on her. That's what made him so dangerous.

Chapter 2

"Twenty five thousand? How the fuck did this happen?" Tony tossed the sheaf of documents onto his desk and strode to the window. The street scene outside wasn't exactly peaceful or calming, but it was infinitely more soothing than the mayhem contained in those pages.
"Someone screwed up, that's how." The quiet, measured tones of his PA belied the direct nature of her words. Isabel Barnard had worked for him for the last ten years, and for his father before that. She knew Tony appreciated plain speaking, and had no objection to it herself. "Your predecessor didn't want to pay out for good legal advice so his head of HR—now your head of HR—managed the case himself. He turned up at the tribunal with incomplete documentation, he wasn't rock solid on the right procedures, he couldn't demonstrate…"
"Okay, okay, I get it. A car crash, right?"
"Right. The tribunal took a coach and horses through our case, found for the claimant on all counts."
Tony surveyed the street below for several more seconds, then turned from the window with a sigh. He scowled again at the papers spread on his desk but the message they contained hadn't improved since the last time he perused them. Dart Logistics, his newly acquired logistics and distribution company had just ended up on the wrong end of an industrial tribunal ruling, and had been ordered to pay the complainant compensation of twenty five thousand pounds to soften the blow of his allegedly wrongful dismissal. As far as Tony could make out his ex-employee hadn't put in a full week's work for nearly four years, and seemed especially averse to Mondays and Fridays, but had still managed to convince the tribunal that he'd been badly treated. At least Tony's firm hadn't been ordered to reinstate the idle slug, so he supposed he should be thankful for that.
"Is there any point in appealing?" He glanced across the desk at Isabel who was leafing through the pile of papers.
She shook her head slowly. "Unlikely. These matters are more concerned with process than justice. The tribunal isn't saying you shouldn't have fired Jeremy Malone, just that you, sorry, the

previous CEO, should have made a better job of it. The warnings weren't recorded properly, Malone didn't have representation when he was interviewed by HR, he wasn't made aware of the necessary standards he had to achieve in order to retain his position. Like I said, process."

"Standards! Just turning up for work and doing a decent job would have done the trick."

His PA shrugged. "There's nothing in here to suggest Mr Malone wasn't good at his job. He just wasn't here enough to show us that."

Tony tunnelled his fingers through his hair, unable to contain his exasperation. "Christ, I know you're right about the process stuff. We all know how these things work. That's why it's so bloody annoying. Twenty five grand, for fuck's sake."

"Yeah. We got the tribunal on a bad day. Might be worth appealing the level of the award, if not the decision…"

"Get our lawyers on it. Meanwhile, I intend to make sure this crap doesn't happen again. You can start by sending the head of HR in to see me. What did you say his name was?"

"Eric Henderson. Been here for five years. Solid enough chap but not really an HR specialist. He's an IT man, but he got human resources tagged on to his department in a cost-saving exercise last year."

"Right. Good result. Twenty five thousand pounds worth of cost saving. Bloody fucking hell."

Isabel stacked the documents into a neat pile and stood. "Quite. I'll ask Henderson to come up, but in fairness I don't think you can really blame him. He was dumped on too."

"I'll be the judge of that. And if Henderson's not the right man for the job we're going to need someone who is."

"I've been thinking about that. I know someone who might suit. Shall I arrange a meeting?"

It was on the tip of Tony's tongue to thank her, and agree to interview whoever she put in front of him. Isabel was good like that, she anticipated his needs and sorted things without needing to be told. But on this occasion, he had an idea of his own he wanted to play with.

"Thanks, but not yet. There's another solution I think I might try first."

"I see. And what's that then?"

"Just an idea. Someone I need to talk to first though."

"Well, don't take too long about it. We need to get this mess under control before we find ourselves with another expensive mistake to deal with. Right. I'll get on to Eric Henderson then. Are you free to see him now?"

"It's as good a time as any. No point putting it off."

Even as Tony muttered the words at his PA's retreating back he knew she was right, as usual. This company was a mess, which had a lot to do with why he'd been able to acquire it so cheaply. It was clear he had some work to do knocking it into shape, but he didn't mind that. He thrived on the challenge. First order of business would be to surround himself with people who he could trust and who were good at their jobs. Isabel was a given. Henderson might turn out to be a square peg in a round hole but he'd soon determine that. Tony himself was a strategist, a gifted corporate visionary and leader, good with people but absolutely no use at all with systems and detail. And that was where his problems seemed to lie.

He sighed. Isabel was right, he was going to need some help here, someone who could get to grips with Henderson's shambles of a department. And he had a feeling he knew the very person. He just needed to convince his old friend.

*****

"You want to what?" Stephen Kershaw lowered his steel grey eyebrows at Tony and glowered at him from under them.

Tony wasn't impressed. He sipped his coffee and met his godfather's stern gaze. "I want to borrow Mrs Richmond."

"She's not a bloody library book. And I'm not lending you my right hand woman."

"Think of it as career development for her. She'll probably be glad of the change, and the challenge if she's half as good as you say."

"She's every bit that good, which is why I need her here. And she has plenty to challenge her running Kershaw Storage, thank you very much. Or if she doesn't, she soon would if I was crazy enough to start loaning out my best staff to the competition."

"I'm not the competition. You're in warehousing, I'm in distribution. We complement each other. If I do well, you do well. And I'm family."

"You're a bloody nuisance, that's what you are. I should have smelled a rat when you were so keen to see me. I don't clap eyes on you for months on end, then suddenly you're in my office, hassling my secretary for an appointment."

"It's been a while, true. We're both busy men. But you owe me a favour, Stephen. Or seven. What about when you had that fire and I let you shift all your undamaged stock into my lorries for three days until you could hire temporary space. Then there was that contract with Linton's—I introduced you and put in a good word, and they turned out to be your best customer to date. And what about the time your operations manager broke both his legs skiing while you were tied up looking after Diana? Who was it who stepped in and ran your company as well as mine for three months until you got sorted out?" Tony paused in his catalogue of good deeds to let the implications sink in. He leaned forward in his seat. "I only want to borrow her. Six months tops."

Stephen's response was an inarticulate grunt.

"How is Diana these days anyway?" Tony knew when and how to press his advantage.

"Good. She's good. The cancer's still in remission so we're hoping it stays that way."

"Me too. Really. Give her my love."

"You could give her it yourself if you'd come round once in a while."

"I will. Soon. So, about Mrs Richmond...?"

"You've never even met her. How do you know you'll get on? She might not be what Dart Logistics needs at all."

Tony sensed the older man's resolve softening. He leaned forward, holding Stephen's gaze as he enumerated the virtues of the renowned Mrs Richmond. "Efficient, forensic eye for detail, meticulous. A degree in law, second degree in business accountancy. Did I miss anything?"

Stephen Kershaw shook his head. "Sounds about right. But she's sharp too, doesn't suffer fools. She can be abrasive. Your people won't take to her, at least not at first."

"I'll smooth all that over. I'm not looking for someone to win popularity contests, and she won't be in an outward-facing role with my customers. What I need right now is someone in my back room to go through my organisation, top to bottom, unearth all the flaws and sloppy practises, point out what needs fixing, and better still fix it for me. She'd have free rein, and my full support."

His godfather eyed him, his expression thoughtful. "You must be worried. What is it you suspect?"

"We have issues in HR for certain, but those are probably superficial and easily fixed with a head of department who knows his stuff. I'm uneasy about my accounts and finance section too, though I can't put my finger on just why. The gap between last year's forecasts and our actual performance was huge, and I'm not sure it can just be explained by unpredictable market forces, or even incompetence at our end. I want someone I can trust crawling all over the figures, someone who can get under the skin of it and tell me what's really going on."

"I see. Well I reckon Mrs Richmond could do that, but you're not having her full time. You can have her for two days a week, if she's agreeable. I'll ask her, but it's her choice. If she's not interested I won't have you hassling her or me. Six months you say? Maximum?"

"Well that was my estimate if she was with me full time…" A determined creasing of the older man's forehead convinced Tony he'd pushed him as far as was prudent. "Okay. Six months, part time. And I'll offer her a bonus, ten percent on top of whatever you're paying her here."

"I doubt the money will make any difference. I'll tell her what you want to discuss and ask her to contact your office, but only if she wants to."

"That'll do me. Thanks." Tony sat back and finished his coffee. He only needed to talk to the woman, surely. He could be persuasive when he set his mind to it.

*****

Anthea rearranged the strap of her satchel-type bag on her shoulder and marched across the gleaming tiled foyer of the offices of Dart Logistics. She was shooting for purposeful, and thought she might have nailed it. The middle aged receptionist smiled up at her from behind her computer. "Can I help you?"

"I'm here to see Anton diMarco please. Anthea Richmond. I have an appointment."

The receptionist offered her another warm smile as she tapped numbers into her keyboard. "I have Anthea Richmond in Reception, to see Mr diMarco." A pause, then, "Of course. I'll send her right up." She returned her attention to Anthea. "You need the second floor. The lift's over there. Mr diMarco's PA will meet you upstairs."

Anthea thanked her and headed for the lift. First impressions do count, and the outward face of Dart Logistics seemed pleasant enough, professional with just the right dash of welcoming to put visitors at their ease. Despite this, as she pressed the call button and waited for the car to arrive she wondered, not for the first time, why she was even bothering with this meeting. She had no intention of agreeing to a secondment here.

The timing couldn't be worse. Stephen's plans for the future of Kershaw Storage were unpredictable, especially since he started dropping big hints about wanting to spend more time with his wife. But even without that complication, she wouldn't be interested. Anthea liked order, she craved certainty. A six month stint in a strange, ailing company, where she knew no one, where she would have to prove herself all over again to yet another sceptical and hostile audience? No thanks. Not for her.

Not happening.

The lift came to a smooth halt at the second floor and the doors glided open. Anthea stepped out to be greeted by another middle aged woman, but where the receptionist on the ground floor had oozed quiet calm, this individual crackled with nervous energy. Anthea half expected to feel a jolt of electricity shoot up her arm as the woman took her hand and shook it.

"Mrs Richmond? So nice to meet you. We've heard so much about you already. I'm Isabel Barnard. I act as PA to Mr diMarco and I'll be looking after you too, if you join us. Which we hope you will, obviously. This way please. Mr diMarco will see you straight away." Anthea followed the woman's bustling figure as she trotted off along the corridor, conscious she hadn't managed to get even one word out. She'd hardly set foot in the place and already her fame seemed to be spreading. Was that a good thing?

It hardly mattered. She wouldn't be joining this firm anyway, helping to prop up this Mr diMarco who seemed incapable of putting his own house in order. She was here out of loyalty to Stephen, nothing else. She was genuinely fond of her employer. He'd had confidence in her and was able to overlook her other shortcomings because she did a damn fine job. Still, she felt indebted to the elderly businessman who'd been able to see past the uptight, driven young woman asking him for a position in accounts. He set her on, and allowed her to hone her natural talents, encouraging her to assume more and more responsibility across all facets of his business. She'd amply repaid his confidence in her in the couple of years she'd worked for him, and in return she knew that Stephen valued her. He respected her. He understood her.

Which was why she was so unnerved now at the prospect of his looming retirement. The next CEO would no doubt find her awkward and gauche. Everyone else seemed to. Her direct, tactless approach would get her into trouble as it always did before. It wasn't that she ever intended to be rude, just that things came out wrong. Her career before Kershaw's was littered with irritated or offended colleagues, complaints, grievances. She dreaded the thought of starting all over with a new boss.

There was an alternative, but that was probably even worse. Stephen had dropped a few hints, and she'd managed to deflect him. Then he'd come right out with it. He wanted her to take over as CEO when he retired. He'd suggested she accept promotion to the role of deputy CEO now, with a view to stepping up in due course. Better still, he'd like her to buy the company and had assured her she'd have no trouble at all raising the cash. Anthea knew that wouldn't be an issue, she could dazzle the company bank manager with her talk of cash flows and revenue projections, and could back all that up with rock solid evidence. They'd be offering her loans until the cash came out of her ears.

Anthea dreaded all of that. She harboured no desire at all to have the top job, to be the one in the public eye, the one who had to deal with their employees face to face, the media, prospective clients. It wasn't that she was without ambition or shunned recognition. She craved all that, had worked hard to build her career and was proud of what she'd achieved. But she was at home with her spreadsheets, her laptop, her policies and procedures. The company ran like a well-oiled machine under her expert control, she loved the quiet, predictable order of it all and knew it was her doing. But the cut and thrust, the chaos of leadership, of scanning the horizon for new opportunities, recognising a chance when she saw it and grabbing it with both hands—that was not for her.

"We're just through here, please." Ms Barnard opened a door and gestured Anthea to go in. "Can I get you something to drink? Tea? Coffee?"

"Thank you. Just a glass of water please." Anthea stepped into the outer office which seemed to be Ms Barnard's domain. Another door at the far end of the room stood ajar.

"Just go straight in. He's expecting you."

Anthea nodded, crossed the office and pushed the second door wide. She entered, a manufactured smile plastered to her face.

The blood drained from her features as the man behind the desk rose to greet her.

"Tony!"

"Mrs Richmond." His slow smile of recognition transformed to one of incredulity, then amusement. He came around the desk toward her, hand outstretched. "How nice to meet you at last. Do please have a seat."

Anthea was rooted to the spot. She stared at him, this man she knew so well, who knew her intimately, this man who was familiar with every contour and hollow of her body, every nerve and muscle. This man who could bring her shuddering to orgasm with just a few precise strokes of his fingers, or drive her to scream her safe word with a twist of his hand.

This man who was her fantasy. Her other world. This man who unleashed her secret self and brought her the relief that kept her sane. He was here, where he had absolutely no business being at all, in her safe, ordered real world.

He would expose her. She'd be humiliated, her carefully constructed fledgling career in ruins.

How had this happened? She'd been so careful, taken no risks, but still…

"Anthea? Thea? Sit, please." His voice was soft but strong, commanding. So him.

Wordless, she sank into a chair at a small meeting table, her mind whirling, desperate to make sense of this turn of events. Tony sat down opposite her.

Moments later Ms Barnard hustled in with a tray bearing a jug of iced water and two glasses. She set that down on the table. If she was conscious of the tension in the room she offered no comment. "I'll be outside if you need me."

"Thank you, Isabel." Tony reached for the jug and filled a glass. He pushed it towards Anthea. "Here. You've had a shock. Take a few sips."

Anthea obeyed, on autopilot now. Something in his voice just brought out that response in her, regardless of the circumstances. In moments she drained the glass, which was refilled straight away. She drank again, then set the remaining water down.

"How did you find me?" Her voice was small, barely a whisper. She experienced a peculiar, detached sense of surprise at how at odds her tone was with her attire. When she dressed for work she was strong, sure, in control and utterly confident. But what came out of her mouth now was her submissive voice, her Wicked Club tone, the one reserved for a different set of circumstances entirely.

"I didn't. At least, not intentionally. I had no idea that Stephen's efficient Mrs Richmond and my gorgeous and sexy Thea were one and the same."

"They're not."

"No?"

"No! I don't, I mean, that's different, at the club. That's not the real me."

"You look pretty real from where I'm sitting."

"Please, can't we just forget about this? I'll go and, and… you don't have to see me again. You can't tell anyone. The club rules say we have to respect privacy. I won't reveal any details, and you mustn't either."

"Whoa, hold it. Why all the fuss? Of course I won't be discussing your—our—private relationship with anyone else. And I certainly hope I will see you again. I hope to see a lot more of you in fact."

"No. That wouldn't do, not at all. I need to keep things private and now, now we…"

"Thea, calm down. This is me, remember. Tony. Your Dom. You can trust me, you know that."

"No, I mean yes. There I do, at the club. But here, I… it won't work. Not at all. I'm sorry. I have to go."

Anthea leapt to her feet, grabbing her satchel from the floor beside her chair. Tony remained seated, made no attempt to delay her.

If Isabel Barnard was surprised that her meeting with Tony diMarco had been such a brief affair, again she gave no sign of it as Anthea charged through the secretary's office looking for all the world as though the flames of Hell were at her heels. The door slammed shut behind her as she broke into a run, heading for the door, the outside.

Safety.

Chapter three

Tony charged across his office in pursuit, then winced at the sound of the outer door shuddering on its hinges. He thought better of chasing Thea through the building and instead strolled as far as Isabel's room. His loyal secretary turned to her boss, leaning against the frame of his office door.

"Went well, then?" Her dry tone caused his eyebrow to lift. "Would you like me to arrange that meeting with my contact now?"

"Could have been worse, I daresay." He levelled a look at her, his determination solidifying. "Thanks for the offer, but I'm not done with Mrs Richmond yet. It just looks like the negotiations are going to be a little more complex than I thought."

Isabel made a sound which he thought might have been a snort, but he chose not to pursue that now. He needed to think.

Back at his desk Tony poured himself a glass of water and turned over the events of the last few minutes in his mind. So, Stephen Kershaw's Anthea Richmond and his own beautiful little sub were one and the same woman. Interesting, and unexpected. She was running now, from him and he suspected from herself too. He wasn't about to let her go, but the situation was fragile to say the least. How best to reel her back in?

He sipped his water and considered the problem, assimilating what he knew about the enigmatic Mrs Richmond.

Mrs? He was as sure as he could be that she wasn't married, but the lady was turning out to be full of surprises. He would have to check.

He cast his mind back to the first time he spotted the beautiful submissive hovering on the fringes of the action in The Wicked Club dungeon. She had been alone that evening, no collar indicating any prior claim, and that surprised him. It was his first visit to the club as he'd only lived in the city for a few weeks, and he could only conclude that the regular Doms in the area were either blind or stupid. Still, their loss. He made a beeline for her and invited her to join him for a drink.

She was enchanting. Intelligent, soft spoken, her submissive mannerisms had his cock standing to attention within seconds. He hoped she hadn't noticed, but couldn't be sure. In the end it didn't matter, they were both here for the same thing, and when she agreed to scene with him that first night he was determined to impress her.

It was just a spanking, but he knew it brought her right to the edge. She didn't ask him to stop, but he was experienced enough to know when she'd had enough. Her bottom was glowing in various shades of crimson and red, heat radiating from her buttocks as he caressed them with his palm. He had leaned over her inert, shivering body and asked her if he could touch her. She had nodded, but he wanted, needed more than that in the way of consent.

"Speak to me, Thea. Tell me."

"Touch me, Sir. Please. I want to come." Her voice had been breathy, laced with need and arousal. He required no further encouragement.

He had slipped his fingers beneath the scrap of lace which passed as a thong and found her slick folds. He stroked her, opening her as she gasped her delight. Tony normally preferred to make his subs wait, he liked them to earn their orgasms, but not on this occasion. He wanted to please this lovely little sub and he knew she craved this. He slid two fingers into her hot, wet pussy, and she started to convulse. He added a third finger, and knew the instant he located her G spot. Her body jerked violently and she squeezed hard as her inner walls contracted. She was close, almost there. He rubbed, murmured something obscene into her ear, and she came.

Afterwards she lay still, a half smile on her lovely lips. It was an intimate moment, and Tony brushed his mouth over hers. She opened her eyes, beamed at him.

"Thank you, Sir. That was perfect."

In Tony's view it was Thea who was perfect. He'd thought so then, and nothing that had happened between them since had altered that opinion. He wanted her, now more than ever. All of her. The question was, how?

*****

Tony sipped his iced water and checked his watch for the third time. Twenty past ten, and still no sign of Thea. She had never been late before, she knew that would be disrespectful and her Dom would not tolerate it. Although Tony knew full well that their encounter in his office two days earlier would have changed everything in Thea's thinking, certainly her frantic reaction gave that impression, their previously agreed arrangement still stood as far as he was concerned. Neither of them had texted the other to change or cancel it. She should be here.

He waited another ten minutes before pulling out his phone and tapping in a curt text.

Where are you, sub?

He hit send, then laid the phone on the low table in front of him as he waited for her response. She didn't keep him waiting long.

You knew I wasn't coming. I told you it was over.

He waited a further fifteen minutes before typing his reply.

You left halfway through our conversation. This is not over. I want to talk to you. You should be here.

The reply was almost instant.

I apologise, Sir. But I can't. Not any more. I'm sorry

Tony waited just couple of minutes before sending his response.

Phone me. Now.

Five minutes passed. He rapped his finger tips on the table, his concern growing. Thea was a spirited sub, she took careful handling, but she was usually obedient. She certainly understood the concept of 'now' and would be under no illusion what that meant. It didn't mean take your time and phone me when you get around to it. He needed to bring her back into line, and he knew her well enough to be aware that her head would be all over the place by now. She had defied him, whether intentionally or not. She was doing it still, and she'd be in knots over it.

The phone rang after eleven minutes.

"Hello, Thea. You took your time."

"I know, Sir. I'm sorry. I just, I needed to think, to work out what I have to say."

"I see. And what do you have to say, Thea?"

"I should have let you know I wasn't going to be there tonight. I assumed you'd realise, after what happened, and I, I…"

"Tell me, Thea."

"I didn't want to make contact with you."

"Why's that, Thea?"

"You scare me."

Her voice had dropped to a whisper, and Tony knew he had to reach her. He was also reasonably certain that it was the circumstances that had frightened her, not him. Thea viewed him with healthy respect which had built over the months they'd scened together. It was the cornerstone of their D/s relationship, and in turn he cherished her trust. She wasn't scared of him, but he could easily see that in her current confusion she might think this.

"I want to see you. Now."

"But, it's late. I'm not dressed. And, I don't want to go to the club."

He noted with satisfaction that she was querying the details, but not refusing to see him. "Where do you live, Thea?"

"I, I prefer not to say, Sir."

"Okay. I'm going to text you my home address. I want you to text me straight back and tell me how long it will take you to get there."

"You want me to come to your house? Tonight?"

"I do. Now. No getting dressed, just come as you are. Immediately. Any questions?"

There was a slight pause, then. "No, Sir. Text me the details please."

*****

Tony opened the door as soon as he heard the tyres crunching across the gravel in his driveway. He watched from his porch as Thea got out of her car and gazed up at him. The four steps leading up to his door helped to create the right air of authority and he watched dispassionately as she approached him.

Her long, dark hair was loose, falling in unrestrained waves around her shoulders. Her calf-length raincoat covered her entirely. She wore flat sandals on her feet, completely at odds with her usual spiky-heeled footwear. He knew her to be almost thirty, but tonight she looked very young, and more than a little lost. Her eyes were rimmed in red, a sign she'd been crying on the way over here. Tony cursed himself. He should have insisted she tell him her address, then he could have sent a cab for her.

"Sir? I got her as quickly as I could, but there are road works…"

"That's fine. You're not late. Come inside." He gentled his tone on purpose, seeking to reassure her. This new twist to their usual arrangement would be unnerving enough for Thea at any time, but given her present state of insecurity and ambivalence toward him he sensed he had to proceed with care. These first moments would be crucial.

He waited as she mounted the steps, then shifted to one side to allow her to walk past him into his house.

"First on the right." He directed her into his dining room. The solid ash table in the centre of the room was bare except for the rattan cane he had placed there earlier, and the leather collar he always insisted she wore when they met at the club. He was well aware these would be the things she would spot the moment she entered and their significance would not be lost on her.

He followed Thea into the room. She was unbuttoning her coat, her gaze locked on the cane. She slid the coat from her shoulders, and he was delighted to see she wore only her bra and panties under it. When she'd told him she wasn't dressed, she meant that literally. And she'd obeyed his instructions to the letter, come just as she was. He stepped forward and took the garment from her, then was gratified and more than a little relieved to watch her sink to her knees before him.

She didn't speak, just knelt, head bowed, her hands resting palms up on her thighs. Her practised submissive posture conveyed far more than words. She wanted, needed, his dominance and it had to be now. She'd seen the cane, knew what he planned to do to her, and she accepted it. Craved it.

The caning was part of his plan, but it had been his intention to talk to her first. That was his primary purpose in insisting on this face to face encounter, but his gut told him to provide for her immediate needs before his own. Tony rarely ignored his Dom instincts.

He picked up the collar and walked around behind her. "Lift up your hair please."

She did as he'd asked. He crouched to fasten the leather around her neck. He stood, his hands resting on her shoulders as she leaned into him.

"I'm going to punish you, Thea. For breaking our arrangement to meet at the club tonight, and also for your bad manners at my office earlier this week. You left before we had finished our discussion."

"Yes, Sir. I shouldn't have behaved as I did." Her voice was low, barely more than a murmur.

"I don't doubt you had your reasons, and I will want to hear them. After." He gave her shoulders a final reassuring squeeze then returned to his position in front of her, one hip hitched on the edge of the table.

Thea followed him with her gaze, never wavering. He recognised the uncertainty in her expression, and the nervousness. But he also saw trust. He could work with that.

"Of course, Sir." Her tone seemed perhaps a little stronger now, and he was encouraged by it.

"Stand up, please and remove your underwear."

Thea got to her feet and reached behind her to unclasp the bra. He took it from her, then held out his hand for her panties too. He left her to stand in the centre of the room, naked, while he deposited her clothes in the hallway outside. He re-entered the dining room and leaned against the table again. At first he said nothing. Instead he watched her for a couple of minutes, during which time she remained absolutely still. He had to hand it to her, she was taking this calmly, like the experienced sub she was. Still, he knew he had drawn it out long enough.

"Go to the end of the table and lean over it. I'd like you to stretch out, please and lift up your bottom for me. You may grip the edges with your hands. Once in position you are not to move until I give permission."

Thea gave a graceful bow of her head, then did as instructed. Tony's cock swelled and twitched in his jeans at the sight of her gorgeous, upturned bottom presented for punishment. Thea did have the most delightful arse, round, curvy, yet firm—the sight of it never failed to affect him.

It had been over a week since they last scened, and no tell-tale marks remained on her body, nothing to indicate the intense physical nature of their relationship. He never saw her between scenes so had no way of knowing how long she usually bore his marks for. He had a sense that was about to change. He hoped so.

"Ten strokes. Four for your no-show tonight, and six for the display of temper in my office. Are you ready?"

"Yes, Sir. I, I think so. And, can I just say, I'm sorry. About tonight and about that other thing. I don't know what happened, I was confused and..."

Ah, some sign of nerves at last. And the start of a conversation he was keen to continue. About time, but first things first. Tony picked up the cane and tried a couple of experimental swishes through the air. He was gratified to note that Thea flinched at the sound. Yes, ten would be enough to discharge her most recent crop of demons. Then she'd be in the right frame of mind to talk to him some more, and to listen.

"Keep your feet on the floor the whole time. You may make as much noise as you like—my closest neighbour is a quarter of a mile away. This will hurt, but I'll be quick. Then you can apologise again, and we'll talk about what happened this week. Okay?"

"Yes, Sir. Thank you."

Tony quirked his lip as he positioned himself behind her. He wondered if she'd feel quite so grateful after he'd striped her bottom for her.

Probably. He hoped.

Thea let out a sharp hiss and went up on her toes when the first stroke landed, hard across both buttocks. Tony waited a few seconds to allow the sensation to sink into her now rigid flesh, only delivering the second when he saw the slight softening of her muscles as she recovered her composure.

She yelped that time, and he watched as the second vivid stripe bloomed across her bum. She was gripping the edges of the table so hard her knuckles were white, but she managed not to move. Tony shifted his stance a little and placed the next two strokes on the lower part of her bottom. Each one brought her back up onto her toes, and now she was whimpering between each blow. He waited a few more seconds then laid a stroke across the back of her right thigh.

Thea screamed, as he'd known she would. Sit spots were the most tender. He moved to the other side and repeated the stroke on her left thigh.

She was sobbing now, her body shaking under the stress. Tony paused to admire the six perfectly defined crimson lines which contrasted sharply with her pale buttocks and thighs. These first marks were all parallel to each other, their positioning precise and accurate. He intended to lay the rest diagonally across them, one on each cheek and thigh. A work of art.

He attended to her right buttock first, eliciting another shrill shriek. Thea's face was turned toward him, resting on the table top, partly hidden behind her wild mane of hair. He could see that her lips were parted slightly. Her tears flowed freely though her eyes were closed. He stroked the tangled mass away from her face, dampening his fingers on her tears. She shifted her head a little, enough to kiss his hand as he caressed her face. On impulse he leaned over and brushed his lips across her temple. He would not usually show any sign of tenderness during a punishment, but this occasion was different. Somehow.

Her lips curled in a soft smile, and she opened her eyes. He smiled back at her. "Almost done."

"Thank you, Sir." Her voice was a faint whisper. He knew she was struggling, this caning was harsh. But she wasn't in distress. She was still with him.

The next stroke landed on her right thigh, crossing the stripe already there.

"Oh, God. Oh Christ, that hurts."

Tony didn't answer, just shifted ready to place the next one.

Thea screamed at the whoosh as he swung the cane through the air, and her whole body jerked when it landed across her left thigh. Tony hadn't increased the severity of the blows, but the cumulative effect was beginning to tell. He was pleased there was only one stroke remaining—much more would have resulted in her safe wording. Not a catastrophe, but he could do without that complication tonight.

"Last one." He waited for her slight nod, then delivered it, sharp and true, cutting a stripe across the two already adorning her left cheek. Thea's final scream echoed around his dining room. She remained spread across his table top, her entire body shuddering. Tony tossed the cane onto the table above her head and stood back to admire the exquisite symmetry of his work.

Thea's breathing was rapid, and her body stiff. Even as he watched, she softened, relaxed. Her death-grip on the edges of the table loosened and her panting slowed.

She opened her eyes and caught his gaze. She offered him a small, apologetic smile. "May I see, Sir?"

"Of course." Tony fished his phone from his pocket and took a quick snap of her beautifully punished arse. He slid the device along the table to her.

Thea took it and perused the picture for a few moments. She turned her head to look at him over her shoulder. "You have a very firm hand, Sir. And accurate too."

"I'm glad you appreciate my efforts. You may stand up when you're ready."

"Thank you, Sir. I'd prefer to stay here for a few more minutes though, if I may."

"No problem. Tea?"

"Perhaps in a little while. I, I don't want you to go anywhere, Sir. Not yet." Despite her increasing composure, her vulnerability in these moments following a severe punishment was apparent. Tony was prepared for it.

"I know that, love. I brought the kettle in here earlier."

"Ah, well then..."

Tony busied himself making her a pot of the fresh Earl Grey he knew she favoured, and was pleased when he saw her ease herself gingerly into an upright position after a couple more minutes. He placed her teacup on the table, next to the discarded cane. Then he took a last look at his proud work on her bottom and thighs before draping a soft blanket across her shoulders and pulling the edges together in front of her. He picked her up and carried her to the low sofa at one end of the room. There he sat, and arranged her in his lap.

"Oh, that's sore, Sir." She wriggled, trying to keep the weight off her tender skin. Tony let her find the most comfortable position before answering.

"Good. Did it do the trick?"

"Yes. I feel much more ... settled now. Thank you. And, I want to apologise if I may, please. For being rude to you, and to your secretary. I would never normally behave like that at work. I was just so surprised. And confused. Scared as well. I never expected to see you anywhere but at the club and I didn't know how to be around you. But—that's no excuse."

Tony considered her explanation for a few moments, as far as it went. Her reaction in his office was too extreme to be explained merely as a reaction to having had a shock, or being confused. Her remark about being scared was interesting. There was more to this, he knew it, and he intended to get to the bottom of what scared her so. For now he was content to take some of what she said at face value.

"It was a shock. I get that. I wasn't expecting to run into you either. I get the impression you don't like surprises much though. Am I right?"

"Yes Sir, I suppose so."

"But you're feeling settled now, you said."

She nodded, so Tony continued.

"That sounds good to me, we can work with settled. You left your tea over there, on the table."

"It's a bit too hot just now anyway, Sir."

"I see. And talking of hot, would you like me to put some cream on your bum?"

She wriggled against him, sending his swollen cock into another twitching frenzy. He needed to conclude this conversation and fuck her soon, for both their sakes.

"In a moment. I'd just like a cuddle right now. If that's alright."

Right, okay then. He dropped a kiss on the top of her head and gathered her in close. Despite having no relationship outside of the club—well, not up until now—there was something about this little sub which just got to him every time.

Several minutes slid by as he held her, breathing in the essence of Thea's musky scent. She would be aroused by the caning, he knew that with bone-deep certainty, and so very fuckable. A punishment always had that effect on her and his cock was issuing its own insistent response to the promise of what the rest of their evening held. But he wasn't led by his dick. Well, not as a rule. First, he had an agenda.

"Let me pass you your tea."

"Mmm, thank you, Sir." She squirmed against his chest.

Tony eased her onto the sofa. "Lie on your stomach. I'll get the cream too."

He placed the teacup within easy reach on a low side table, and proceeded to re-position her across his lap. The blanket was discarded to lie in an untidy heap on the floor as he traced the still-vivid marks on her bum and thighs.

"Do you know how beautiful this is, Thea?"

"I think I do, Sir. At least, I hope so."

"You know so."

She shook her head. "I'm not sure what I know, any more."

"Oh? Shall I tell you what I know then?" He uncapped the tube of anti-inflammatory cream and dispensed a generous line onto his fingertips.

"I'm not sure I want to hear this."

"Oblige me anyway. Are you listening, Thea?"

She turned her head toward him, her expression one of surprise. "Of course."

"I mean *really* listening. Taking in what I'm saying to you."

"I… think so, Sir. Oh, that's cold."

Tony smoothed cream into the delicate skin of her buttocks, massaging slowly, gently as the salve was absorbed.

"Wimp. Stop wriggling. So, where was I? Ah, right. What do I know, about you?" He paused, she seemed disinclined to add any further comments so he continued. "One, you're a sweet, responsive little subbie. Incredibly sexy, and something of a pain slut on the quiet. I look forward to our scenes, and I've pushed you hard in the months we've played together. I've challenged your boundaries and mine. You have courage, an inner confidence that I've watched grow over the time I've known you, and an almost limitless capacity to trust. Does this sound like you, Thea?"

He squeezed out another helping of cream and proceeded to apply it to her left thigh, relishing the almost imperceptible shiver that ran through her slim body at his touch. She was hurting, and loving the pain. And concentrating hard on his words. He waited for her response.

"I used to be much more nervous, that's true. Before I met you. I do trust you. Completely."

Ah, important progress.

"Nervous how? About your kink, about being submissive? Or more generally?" He took care to keep his tone low and even. He wanted to coax more from her.

"About being a submissive, I suppose. I mean, I always knew, from being quite young, but it has only been in the last year or so that I've been able to properly enjoy it. And that's mostly because of you. I tried with other Dom's once or twice but it felt all wrong. I couldn't relax. But with you it's different. It always was, right from that first time. I…like you."

"I like you too. Very much. Do you still scene with any other Doms, Thea?"

He knew the answer to that one, but wanted to hear her acknowledge it. Since meeting Thea his own appetite for playing with other submissives had waned considerably, but there had been no suggestion of exclusivity in their relationship. He suspected that was another thing that was about to change.

"No, of course not. Only you, Sir."

"Why of course not? You only wear my collar on those evenings we're together."

"I don't want to. I couldn't. Another Dom might, might… I just don't. That's all."

"Okay. Good. I've played with different subs, but not recently. And I'm happy to keep it that way. Just you, for as long as we both agree that's what we want. Do we have a deal?"

"I'd like that, Sir. Thank you. Will I get to wear your collar all the time now?"

"Would you like to?" Tony held his breath. He hadn't anticipated this, but now the subject had come up he was remarkably relaxed at the prospect. A collared sub was a responsibility to be sure, and implied a long-term commitment but he believed Thea would be worth it. It was simple enough for him—he wanted her. He felt on reflection that she probably needed the security, the structure and the sense of certainty that his collar would offer her. It would ground her in a way nothing else could. It would appeal to her psyche, and complete the circle for her. If she was ready to accept it.

"I would, Sir. I'd like to be yours. Just yours."

Tony tapped the heavy, studded leather band encircling her neck. "I doubt this would go too well with your business suits though. And it wouldn't be comfortable for wearing all the time."

Her expression fell, she appeared disappointed. He smiled and brushed his lips across her forehead.

"I'll provide you with a more decorative one then. Something—unobtrusive. But you'll understand its significance? Yes?"

"Yes Sir, Thank you."

"So, in the circumstances, are you prepared to tell me where you live? And I do feel compelled to ask about Mr Richmond?"

"What? Oh, right. That was silly. I was just… confused earlier. Babbling. I live in that warehouse conversion, you know, the Old Flax Mill. By the river."

"Very nice. Upmarket."

"It's tiny, not much more than a studio really. But yes, it is nice."

"And Mr Richmond?"

"I'm not married. I never have been. It just sounds more professional, and, and businesslike."

"How so?"

"If people, colleagues, think I'm married they won't expect me to socialise, or anything."

"And what's the problem with socialising? You like to have fun, I know that."

"Fun with you, yes. No one else."

"I don't just mean kinky fun. What about friends? People to chat with by the copier? Or to go for a drink with after work?"

"I don't drink, and I have a photocopier in my office."

He tapped her bum, but the slap was playful this time. "Don't be obtuse, Thea. Why don't you socialise?"

"I'm no good with people. People don't like me. I have no sense of humour, and I'm boring. They respect me though, because I'm good at my job. That's what I want. It's *all* I want. It's enough."

"I'll agree you're good at your job. That's why I want you working for me. But the rest of what you just said is crap."

"No it isn't. How would you know anyway? You don't know me…Aagh!

Tony brought the stream of self-doubt to an abrupt end with a sharp slap to her bottom. There was nothing playful about this one. "As long as you're wearing my collar you'll dump that rubbish. You're a lovely, desirable, intelligent woman, whether in a dungeon or a boardroom. Remember it. And live like it. You *will* have friends at Dart Logistics, starting with me, and with Isabel. We'll work out from there. At Kershaw's you can start with Stephen, but I wouldn't mind betting there'll be plenty more once you drop the frosty 'keep out' signs."

"It's not so simple. And with respect, Sir, you don't know me outside of—what we do together."

He was amused, and interested, to note that the threat of further punishment to her very sore behind was not sufficient to dispel the note of defiance in her voice. His little kitten had claws. She didn't show them in her submission, but they were certainly in evidence when her head shifted into her professional life. He wanted to see more of the elusive 'Mrs Richmond'.

"So tell me then. But without the self-put-downs. You can start by telling me what it is you do well. Why do your colleagues respect you?"

She considered for few moments, then, "I'm thorough, efficient. I work hard. I get things right, you know, the details. People can rely on me. I'm a qualified lawyer, and I have a finance diploma too. I know how a business should run."

"All true. Stephen told me all of that. He's very pleased with you. That's why I want you in my company."

"But, I don't know anyone there. How would I manage? People won't listen to what I say. You'll be disappointed."

"I somehow doubt that. And they *will* listen to your ideas because you're good. You know what you're talking about. And because you'll have the authority to insist my heads of department do as you suggest. I want my shit sweeping into a pile, Mrs Richmond—I think I'll continue to call you that, it suits you. And you're just the woman to do it. I need your help. Please."

"I can't. I just can't. Really."

"If you're wearing my collar twenty four seven, I can instruct you to do this. You will obey me, Thea."

She wriggled from her position across his lap and knelt on the floor in front of him. Tony allowed her to go. Still naked but for the collar, her posture was one of total submission. Even so he knew the battle taking place within. He could almost hear the clash of steel and roar of cannon fire as her inner personas slugged it out. She tilted up her chin to meet his gaze.

"Thea obeys. Not Mrs Richmond."

He leaned forward, his face on the same level as hers. "But they are one and the same. Thea Richmond, my submissive, my corporate services director. I need both of you. And you need me." She would have looked away, but he cupped her chin with his palm. "Don't you Thea?"

The ticking of the clock above his fireplace was the only sound as he held her gaze. He watched as emotions danced across her features—panic, dismay, bewilderment. Then acceptance, resignation, and at last, the determined glint he sought.

"Yes, Sir. Very well, I'll try."

"Thank you, that'll do for me. I appreciate it. Very much." He leaned forward the couple more inches needed to brush his lips across hers. "So, I've had the pleasure of Thea in the dungeon at The Wicked Club, and here in my dining room now as well. I can tell you I'm very much looking forward to seeing Mrs Richmond go to work in my boardroom. But who will I see in my bedroom I wonder?"

"You want me to sleep here tonight? With you?"

"Yes."

"Why?"

"Because I want to fuck you. Then I reckon we both need to get some sleep. And tomorrow I want to talk to you about your new duties at Dart Logistics." He stood and offered her his hand. "Come to bed with me. Please."

Thea took his hand and would have followed him from the room, sedate and obedient, a truly chastised and repentant sub. Tony had other ideas. The moment she grasped his hand he scooped her from the floor and carried her from the room. He took the stairs two at a time and strode along the hallway with her in his arms. He shouldered open his bedroom door and laid her on his bed, chuckling when she rolled onto her stomach.

"Are you offering me your arse, girl?"

"If you want it, Sir. Yes, of course."

"Hold that thought while I get some lube."

Chapter four

What on Earth just happened? How did I end up here, a collared sub? Tony's collared sub. Shit!
Thea's head was whirling as she stretched out on her Dom's bed, waiting for him to re-emerge from the bathroom. Despite the inner turmoil raging within, one certainty presented itself, head and shoulders above the rest of her teeming thoughts.
This is good. This is safe. This is where I want to be.
Just hang on to that, and the rest will be okay. Surely.
"You look good there, Thea."
She turned her head at his voice, gratified to note that he was now naked too. And looking very fine with it. Tony had rarely undressed at the club so despite their intimacy she was not especially familiar with his body. Parts of it, yes. But not usually the whole lot, on display. She stared. And stared some more.
Tony obliged her by walking around the room, adjusting lamps. He grinned at her.
"I do hope you're not going to drool on my bedding, Thea. Though on second thoughts…"
"I'm sorry. It's just that I'm not used to you… Not that I mind. It's lovely, really. You are I mean. Lovely."
"So are you, little sub. And I really should have brought you back here before."
"I might not have agreed to come, Sir. We always kept the club and—everything else—separate. I liked it that way."
"I know, and we can talk about why that was. Later. Right now…"
He tossed a tube of lubricant, a bullet vibrator, and three condoms onto the pillow beside her head. "I want you to kneel up and spread your knees as wide as you can. Then lean forward and rest your face on the pillow. Do I need to tie your hands?"
"No Sir, but I'd like you to."
"Leather cuffs okay?"
Thea nodded, and knelt up in the centre of the mattress while he opened one of his bedside drawers and found a pair of cuffs. He fastened one to each of her offered wrists, then gestured for her to place her hands behind her. He snapped the fasteners together to

secure her, then laid a hand on her shoulder to indicate she should lean forward.

Thea made herself comfortable, her cheek pressed against the crisp cotton of the duvet, her bum poised at Tony's eye level as he stretched out on one elbow behind her.

"So beautiful. So hot and wet, and pink as a cherry." He punctuated his remarks by drawing the flat of his palm along her moistening pussy, then dipping two fingers inside her cunt. "Ah yes, very wet. But I still think we need to warm you up a little more. What do you think, Thea?"

"That sounds nice, Sir." She squeezed around him as he drew his fingers back, then drove them deep again, twisting inside her.

"Nice? I guess I'll settle for that for now but I'll be shooting for something closer to fucking wonderful. You'll come for me, as soon as I touch your clit. But not before. Is that understood?"

Thea sighed, grimacing to herself. No matter how often he put her through these paces, she never found orgasm control easy. Her lack of self-discipline invariably earned her a spanking, and her bottom was already very sore,

"Thea?" Tony's voice had softened. He was so adept at picking up on her fears, before she spoke them aloud.

"I'll try Sir, but it's so difficult. And I don't want you to be angry, or spank me. It hurts…"

His finger-fucking had slowed to a sweet, gentle caress.

"Sweetheart, I won't be angry. Whatever happens, I'll know you tried. Do you need me to help you?"

"Help me? How can you…?"

"If you feel you're going to come and can't hold back, just say yellow. I'll stop, give you a chance to calm down. How does that sound?"

"Thank you, Sir. It sounds—lovely."

"Okay, I'm going to lube your arse and get you loosened up, ready for me. I don't want you getting bored though, so I think we'll put the bullet inside your pussy." He thrust again with his fingers, as though she required further clarification as to where the vibrator would be going. "On full, naturally. I want to be sure I have your attention."

Thea groaned. This was going to be intense.

Tony withdrew his hand and reached for the bullet. Then he used his moisture-coated fingertips to part the lips of her sleek, wet pussy.

"Hmm, very slippery here. You really are a randy little slut, Thea. I've hardly touched you." As he spoke he slid the toy between her pussy lips and pressed firmly. It slid into her receptive cunt and Tony followed with his fingers to ensure it was exactly where he intended to place it. "I want this right up against your G-spot, girl. Tell me when it is."

"Oh, God…"

"Thea, tell me."

She jerked as the device whirred to life, just a faint humming at first, but sending vibrations right through her quivering pussy.

"I… not yet, a little higher…" Despite her trepidation, lying to Tony was unthinkable. She clenched as he adjusted the position slightly. "Yes! Oh, God, there."

"Thank you. Now you can concentrate on that while I do my thing here." He slid his fingers from her pussy to switch his attention to her arse.

Thea had had plenty of practice in the months she'd scened with Tony and instinctively loosened as he pressed the tip of his middle finger against her rear opening. He slid inside, swirling his fingertip within to ease the tension in the ring of muscle there. It felt good. Intimate, caring. Tony's impact play could be painful, his punishments definitely so, but he never hurt her by accident. Thea knew he would take all the time needed to prepare her, and that was the problem. Her inner walls were already starting to convulse as the vibrator sent wave after wave of sensual pulsing through her helpless pussy.

"Sir, please. Yellow."

"Already? We'll be here all night at this rate. Still, I'm not going anywhere…" As he spoke he slid a finger into her to hit the off switch and the relentless pulsing ceased.

"Thank you. May I have a drink of water please?"

"Of course." The bed dipped as he stood up. There was the sound of a tap running in the ensuite next door. Thea knew he would be washing his hands. Tony was always so careful about hygiene and her wellbeing. He came back to the bed carrying a small bottle of still water, the top already snapped off. Thea pushed herself upright as he held it to her lips, swallowing several mouthfuls of the cool liquid.

"Enough?"

"Yes. Thank you."

Tony re-capped the bottle and placed it on the bedside table. "Are you ready to continue?"

Thea nodded, and leaned forward again.

This time he lubed his fingers before slipping two into her arse. He had to exert more pressure, but it wasn't painful. It was tight, and it was clear to her he intended to move on fast now, but still he didn't hurt her. When his fingers were fully inserted he used his other hand to re-start the bullet, and she knew this time he'd put it on the next setting up. The vibrations were harder, more compelling, but the impact was less intense. She realised the device had shifted, probably when she knelt upright again. It was no longer applying the stimulation direct to her G-spot. She could manage this, She'd be fine. Except…

"Sir, it's moved. You'll need to put it back against my G-spot."

"Thank you, Thea." He slipped his fingers back inside her and repositioned the toy. The result was as she anticipated—exquisite agony.

"Please be quick, Sir. This is so hard. I can't…"

"Relax, love. You're doing fine. And if you need to stop again, we will."

His quiet voice was in odd contrast to the demanding throb of the vibrator, working its magic inside her body. Its sexy timbre grounded and calmed her, and Thea knew this would be good. The 'fucking wonderful' he'd mentioned earlier might just be within her grasp after all.

Relaxing, she sighed as he inserted a third slick finger into her arse. It wouldn't be long now.

She was almost at the point of calling for another time out when Tony pulled his fingers from her now unresisting rear hole. There was the snap of a condom pack tearing, then the head of his cock was there, at her entrance.

"Push back against me, Thea. Now."

She obeyed, and his cock breached her arse. His penetration was easy, it felt good. So good. He paused for a few moments, and Thea rolled her hips to adjust the fit, then pressed against him again.

"So eager, little sub." His low chuckle was warm and Thea basked in his sensual approval. He thrust hard to drive his cock the rest of the way in, then held still as her body re-shaped around him.

"Doing okay still?" His palms bracketed her hips, holding her against him.

"Yes Sir. It feels so good. But I need to come. Can I…"

He leaned forward, reaching around and under her. The pad of his finger connected with the top of her clit and he rubbed hard.

Thea let out a shriek of sheer joy as her body convulsed. Tony continued to caress her clit as the bullet pulsed waves of sensual delight the length of her pussy.

"So good, sweetheart, so tight. I can feel that too."

"Sir… oh," Thea's fingers clenched and unclenched in the small of her back as her orgasm gripped. Tony released the clips holding her wrists together and she stretched her arms in front of her, grasping handfuls of the duvet to crush in her fists.

Tony pulled back, then thrust again, burying his cock in her arse. Thea's own release was receding, but she let out a moan, then another as he picked up a demanding rhythm. First his strokes were long and straight, claiming his place inside her. Then he shortened them, rapid, teasing, the head of his cock plunging those first couple of tantalising inches.

"More, please Sir, More. Harder…"

Tony shifted and Thea collapsed to the bed, his weight on top of her. Helpless, pinned in place, she felt utterly his. He lengthened his strokes again, each one driving balls-deep into her. All the while he maintained the constant rubbing on her sensitised clit, and she was suddenly caught up in the rush of another climax. Thea's body tightened, tensing, bracing until he pushed her past the point of no return and her wits scrambled again.

This time though he was with her. A low grunt, a muffled oath, and his cock lurched inside her one last time. Then he was still, his weight on his arms as his semen pumped into the condom.

*****

"Usually you get dressed and I call you a cab at this point." Tony nuzzled Thea's tousled hair, inhaling the musky aroma of sated, thoroughly fucked submissive.

"Mmm. This is better, Sir. As long as you don't mind. I mean, if you want me to leave…" Thea nestled against him, her bottom tucked into his groin. Tony's arms were around her, his palm caressing her breast.

"Have I given that impression, little sub?"

"No, Sir. Not really."

"Get some sleep then. In the morning I intend to fuck you until you can't think straight. Then we need to talk business."

"I don't believe that would be a good idea, Sir. The talking business I mean. Not the fucking. Not if I'm not thinking straight."

"I expect you'll manage. If you find yourself struggling another spanking will help to focus your ideas."

"Thank you, Sir. I expect it will. Perhaps you should do that anyway. Just to be certain."

"As long as you're wearing my collar I can promise you all the spanking you need. And some. Now get some sleep."

*****

"This is a nice house. Have you lived here long?"

Tony glanced up from his newspaper. Thea was framed in the dining room doorway, looking utterly delightful in his discarded T shirt from the previous evening. It reached her mid-thigh, leaving a seemingly endless expanse of tanned, slim leg for him to admire. Her ensemble was completed by the studded collar which he had offered to remove before she slept. She'd asked to keep it on.

His cock swelled, springing instantly to life. He was glad of the loose sweatpants he'd dragged on when he left their bed earlier.

Thea had been sound asleep, her hair spread over his pillow, the smooth expanse of her back inviting him to touch, to caress. He hadn't though. She needed plenty of rest if she was to live up to his plans for her later.

He offered her a good-morning smile as he answered. "A while. Ten years or so."

"Why such a big place if you live alone? You *do* live alone?" She frowned at him, her expression uncertain.

"I do, Thea. And I like to spread out."

"Me too. Live alone I mean. I prefer that…"

Tony stood and went to her. He dropped a kiss on her lips. "Is that your way of telling me you don't intend to move in with me?"

"What? No! I mean…"

He grabbed her hand and led her back along the hallway and into the kitchen.

"Oh God, that was so rude. I mean, you haven't even… I'm not assuming, I just…" Thea followed him, obedient as ever despite her confused babbling.

"Have a seat. Tea?" He gestured at one of the tall stools tucked under the worktop. As he busied himself with the kettle and teabags he watched her from the corner of his eye.

Thea clambered onto the stool and perched awkwardly. She nodded in response to his question. Her knees were tucked in front of her, but pressed together to prevent a stray glimpse of her delightfully smooth pussy. He considered asking her to spread her legs, but decided to allow her to drink her tea first. There would be time enough later for recreational pursuits.

He placed the teapot in front of her, and a cup. He made coffee for himself, instant, from a jar. He noted that her hands were unsteady as she poured, and wondered why she was so nervous this morning. Last night, yes, that made sense. But now?

"What's on your mind, Thea?"

"Nothing. I'm fine." Her response was just a little too fast, too emphatic.

"Thea, we'll get nowhere if you don't tell me the truth. I'll ask you just once more." There was no need to elaborate on the likely consequence if she continued to evade. He noted her slight flush and the agitated chewing of her lip. He was tempted to kiss it, but felt that might ruin the stern image he was at pains to cultivate here.

"I'm sorry, Sir. I was just wondering, about the collar..." she paused to finger the leather band, then glanced at him, "... and, being employed in your company too. How will it all work? I mean, I know I'll be your submissive here and I know what that means. But at the office...?"

"I intend to respect your privacy outside of our D/s relationship, Thea. You can be Mrs Richmond at work, and no one need even know we have a personal connection too. Even if we do decide to share that information, the exact nature of our relationship will remain private. That's the way I prefer it too."

"Will you expect me to scene with you here? In your house? Or will we still meet at the club?"

"Both I imagine. I intend for you to spend a lot of time here though. I'll get you a key cut." He leaned in to cup her cheek in his palm. "Thea, I know you feel vulnerable, maybe a little confused right now. You accepted my collar with hardly any discussion, or planning, and now you're wondering what the Hell you've let yourself in for. Am I right?"

"Maybe. It's all a bit—overwhelming."

"Second thoughts?"

"No! No Sir, definitely not." She shook her head, emphasising her denial. "I wanted this. You. I've known that, almost from the first time we scened together. I just didn't think it was possible though. Not and keep my other self, my real-life self, separate."

"This, you and me, is real life too, Thea."

"Yes, I know that. But it's different. I wouldn't want people I work with to know that I love to be whipped. Or that I like having a plug in my arse. Or, well, everything really."

Tony laughed out loud, delighted with her frankness. "Shit, neither would I. That *would* cause some talk around the photocopier. But you must realise that most people who like a little kink prefer to keep their preferences private. That's fine, and not the same as being ashamed of what we enjoy. Not everyone outside our lifestyle gets it, people can be judgemental. I get that you prefer to avoid complications, and it's no one's business but ours in any case. So, we're agreed on that much. What I don't really get though is your insistence on keeping Thea and Mrs Richmond totally separate. And your blind panic last week when you came face to face with me. You were terrified, and I can't work out why. I hadn't said I was going to out you, and there was no reason to suppose I would. I had as much to lose as you, probably."

"You? What would you have to worry about? People take you seriously. You own your own company, for Heaven's sake. What would it matter what anyone thinks of you?"

"Are you saying that people don't take you seriously? Why would you think that?"

"It's always harder for women. In business. You have to be tough. And single minded. No distractions and definitely no scandal. I can't afford to let anyone find out. I just can't."

"Sweetheart, no one's going to find out from me. But even if they did, we'd weather it. We're consenting adults, we can do as we like."

"No! No, you don't understand." She shook her head, vehement in her denial.

"Then tell me, Thea. Make me understand."

"I'm a private person. I always have been. The way I behave when we're at the club. Here, last night. That's not the real me."

"It sure looked like you."

"Don't make fun of me. Please." Her eyes glittered with tears about to fall, but Tony resisted the temptation to comfort. In his experience tears were an honest response from a submissive, and that was what he most required from her now. She would have nowhere to hide.

"You and I share somewhat singular tastes, Thea. But what we do harms no one—including ourselves—so we have nothing to feel ashamed of. Mrs Richmond, Thea, both are different facets of one beautiful woman. Keep your private life private by all means, but don't deny what, who you are. Accept your submission, love it as I do. Most important, don't lie to yourself, and most certainly don't lie to me."

"I don't mean to be dishonest. It's just—hard."

"It doesn't have to be. Let me prove it to you."

"How? How will you do that?"

"Come to work for me. Be my colleague in the office, and my submissive here. Or at the club. Or at your apartment if you prefer.

Let me into your other side, allow me to know all of you. Blur the edges, and see what happens."

"I suppose I already started to do that. By coming here last night."

"Why did you come?"

"Because you ordered me to. I needed to obey. I needed…"

"You needed a bit of Sir time? Yes?"

"Yes." Her voice had dropped to a whisper. "I never felt like that before."

"You never actively defied me before."

"No, Sir. I think now I was looking for a reaction from you. I needed you to take control. Are you still angry?"

Now he did relent. Reaching for her he pulled her to him for a hug. He dropped a kiss onto her hair. "No, and I wasn't angry last night either. As you say, you needed the discipline. You got it. We move on."

"Thank you, Sir."

"And talking of moving on, what do you want to do today? Do you have any plans?"

Still in his arms she tipped up her chin to look at him. "I usually do my shopping at the weekend, clean my apartment. That sort of thing."

"Very commendable. Do you fancy a change? I thought we might go bowling."

"We … what?" Her face was a picture, her expression one of absolute incredulity. It was all he could do not to laugh out loud. He really did need to widen her horizons.

"Ten pin bowling. Then something to eat. Or maybe we could see a film. Not Fifty Shades though—my delicate sensibilities won't stand it."

"You want to go out. With me?"

"Yes. Definitely. First though I'll drive you home and you can get some clothes. And whatever else you might need because you'll be staying here again tonight. We'll have a good time, get to know each other a bit more. Then we'll come back here and I'll brighten up those stripes on your bum before I fuck you. Does that sound like a plan?"

"I've never been bowling."

"No? Then we need to rectify this situation without delay. Finish your tea and put your raincoat back on. You can check the cinema listings on your phone, in the car."

Chapter Five

Thea was laughing as they ran up the steps to his front door, her raincoat draped over both their heads to keep off the rain.
"Beginners luck, that was all. You just kept fluking strikes." Tony tapped her on the bum as he dug in his pocket for the door key.
Thea was irrepressible. "Three! I got three strikes in a row. How many points was that?"
"Fuck knows. No one knows how to add up bowling scores any more, not since it all got automated. Like I said, you got lucky."
"I won. I beat you by…" She fished the printout from the back pocket of her jeans. "… thirty seven points. Wow, imagine that!"
"Yeah, imagine." He unlocked the door and they hurried in out of the rain. Tony took the coat and hung it on the bottom of his banister to drip onto the tiles in his front hallway. "I intend to exact my retribution now. Strip, please."
"What, now?"
Tony arched an eyebrow, all the confirmation she required. Thea unbuttoned her blouse. He watched her slip the garment off, then undo the buttons on her jeans.
"Get naked, and wait for me in the dining room. I expect you can remember the way." He turned on his heel and marched away from her in the direction of the kitchen.
Thea wasted no time in removing the rest of her clothing, leaving everything folded on the bottom step. She placed her bag alongside the neat stack of her garments, then made her way along the hallway, and entered the first door on her right. The table was clear this time, apart from the leather collar. She wasn't sure if this was a good sign or not. For want of more detailed instructions she sank to her knees to wait.
Tony followed her into the room a couple of minutes later. She kept him in her peripheral vision as he dumped a selection of wooden spoons onto the table. She had last seen those spoons in the kitchen drawer and had thought they would come in useful. It seemed Tony was there ahead of her. They fell with a loud clatter, and she flinched despite her contentment at what she knew would

soon happen. This evening was progressing very nicely, in her view, the perfect end to one of the most enjoyable days she could recall.

Tony picked up the collar. "Could you lift up your hair, please, Thea?"

She did as he asked, experiencing a bone-deep sensation of bliss as he fastened the thick band around her neck. Symbolic of his mastery of her, the collar helped her to settle into her submissive mind-set too.

Tony squeezed her shoulder, then crossed the room and opened a drawer in the sideboard. He withdrew several sheets of paper, which he laid on the table next to the spoons. Thea watched him, puzzled.

"May I ask what those are, Sir?" She would never usually question him during a scene, but this seemed odd. Thea liked the familiar, she preferred no surprises.

"Of course you may. It's your contract."

"My contract? But we already negotiated our limits. We talked, we're always talking. Why do we need to write it down?"

He turned to her, his smile deceptively soft. "Not a BDSM contract. As you say, we talk those issues through. This is your contract of employment, Mrs Richmond. At Dart Logistics. Or perhaps it's better described as your consultancy brief since you won't technically be my employee."

Thea was nonplussed. "What? Now? I prefer to read it later. At home, or at the office."

He shook his head. "No. You'll read it here and now. And you'll make notes." He tossed a pen from his jeans pocket on top of the pile of papers. "I expect to see comments, and questions. Would you get on with that, please?"

"If we're to have a business discussion, perhaps I ought to get dressed…" She peered at him, confused. And upset. Was this some sort of rejection? Why? What had she done wrong?

"Did I not instruct you to strip, less than ten minutes ago?"

"Well, yes. But…"

"In that case you can be certain I have no wish to watch you get dressed again just yet. Please stand up. Mrs Richmond. Come to the table and read this contract. Now."

"I don't want to. Can I look at it later?"

His gaze hardened. She had seen that look before. Not often, but enough to recognise what was coming next.

"Thea, on your feet. Now. Bend over the table."

Still reeling from the conflicting thoughts ricocheting around her head, punishment was at least familiar territory, though Tony was not usually so unpredictable. Thea got to her feet and made her way to the table. She leaned on it, looking back over her shoulder at Tony.

He selected one of the spoons and slapped the palm of his left hand with it. "Bend over, arse in the air. You'll be getting two slaps, one on each side. For questioning my perfectly clear instructions. Then I'll tell you again what I want you to do, and I hope this time you won't find it necessary to prevaricate. Are you ready?"

"Sir, I…"

"Are you ready, Mrs Richmond?"

Thea gave a sharp nod and lowered her torso onto the table top. Her breasts flattened against the cool, smooth oak as she lifted her bottom up for a punishment she didn't come close to understanding. This was developing into a scene she was finding more challenging than anything Tony had subjected her to at the club, and it had come out of nowhere. She was confused, off balance, desperately uneasy. Scared even. But even so, two strokes wasn't much. She could handle that.

"Aagh!" The first slap sent her to her toes, the pain burning through her left buttock. The stripes from yesterday's caning were still slightly sore, but pleasantly so. This paddling with Tony's kitchen implements would rekindle that tenderness, and she knew there would be nothing pleasant about these sensations. He seemed really pissed off with her.

She managed to restrain her cries to a sharp hiss when he landed the second stroke on the right side. She was sure he'd spanked her as hard as he could, and it bloody hurt. She couldn't tolerate much more if he was set on continuing like this.

"Stand up." His tone was curt, dripping with authority. Thea pushed herself up on her hands and turned to face him. Tears blurred her vision.

"Do you feel more inclined to do as I say now, or should I repeat the lesson?" His expression was cold, his words clipped.

Thea's confidence shrivelled. What was happening? She nodded and reached blindly beside her for the documents. "May I sit to read them?"

"No. You'll stand at the table. I want you to place your hands on it and lean over, your feet spread as wide as you can. You'll read your contract whilst showing me your pussy. And you'll continue to read, and concentrate on what's written there, regardless of what I do to you. Is that understood?"

"I don't think I can, Sir. Concentrate, I mean. Not like this."

"Why not? The contract is written in plain enough English. Would you like your reading glasses perhaps?"

"I do wear glasses for reading, Sir."

"You have them with you, I trust?"

"They're in my bag, Sir. I left it in the hallway, with my clothes."

"Go and get them please, then get back in here. Be quick about it."

Grateful for the chance of a short respite in which to collect her thoughts, yet at the same time unwilling to be out of Tony's presence for more than the few moments it would take to retrieve her glasses, Thea whirled with a sob. She ran from the room and back along the hallway to the bottom of the stairs. A quick rifle through her bag located the spectacles. She rushed back into the dining room, her glasses case clutched in her fist.

Tony was exactly where she had left him, lounging against the table, the wooden spoon still in his hand. He caressed the implement, as though contemplating the prospect of using it again. Thea clenched her buttocks, her mouth dry as she removed her glasses from their case and perched them on her nose.

"Is that better?" His tone was almost conversational. Almost.

"Yes, Sir. Thank you."

"Adopt the position I described to you then, and start reading. You can make notes in the margins."

"Sir, I don't want to do this. I can't."

"I believe you can. And I'd like you to try please. You can take as long as you need, but you will have read and understood every word of that contract before you leave this room. Now may I suggest you make a start, or be prepared to present your bottom for further punishment? It'll be four strokes if I have to remind you again about obedience."

Thea turned to face the table and pulled the sheets of paper towards her. She flicked through them, counting. Just five sheets. She could manage to read and take in five pages, surely. She drew in a deep breath, held it for several seconds, then leaned forward. She widened her stance, spreading her thighs as far apart as she was able, and arched her back. If she was doing this, she would make every effort to ensure her Dom had no further cause for complaint.

Thea read through the first few lines quickly. Nothing unusual, just the general terms naming the company concerned and the principal parties involved in this agreement. Herself, Althea Richmond, and Anton diMarco. *Tony. Sir to her.* The next section outlined her principal duties at Dart Logistics, the purpose of her secondment there. She moved on to the next section, then yelped as Tony parted her pussy lips with his fingers.

"Did I hurt you?"

"No, Sir. I'm sorry."

"Please continue reading." He plunged three fingers deep into her drenched pussy. Despite her confusion and discomfort, there could be no mistaking Thea's arousal at being made to pose for him in this way.

She closed her eyes, unable to help herself, and clenched her inner walls around his thrusting fingers.

"Mrs Richmond, are you concentrating?"

"Yes Sir. At least, I'm trying to. But it's not easy when you do that."

"I suggest you check the key terms one more time, Mrs Richmond. I will expect you to comply with the terms of this contract once we've agreed it."

Something in his tone warned her. Fighting off the impact of his skilled fingers as they continued to caress her inner walls, Thea re-read the paragraph she just finished. And this time she spotted it. She was to be seconded to Dart Logistics for a remuneration of half her usual salary. This wasn't what she had understood would be the deal.

"Sir, this figure here…"

"If there are any amendments required please note those in the margin and move on. And pay better attention to the rest. I won't prompt you again, and you'll have to live with any mistakes you might make."

Thea bristled. Mistakes. She didn't make mistakes. At least, not of this sort. All her colleagues were agreed on one thing, Mrs Richmond's attention to detail, to the fine print, was legendary. She picked up the pen and scribbled a note alongside the incorrect clause and figure, then gave her head a quick shake to clear her lust-fogged senses. She focused again on the sheet before her.

She found nothing untoward in the rest of that first sheet, and turned it face down on the table next to the pile of unread pages. She heaved a sigh of relief when Tony slid his fingers from her body and stepped away. The respite was short-lived.

Tony returned to the table and placed a saucer on top of her face-down sheet. Thea's heart sank when she saw what it contained.

A long finger of peeled ginger root, a deep groove carved into the flesh about a third of the way along.

"We haven't used figging in our play up to now, but I'm sure you know what it entails, Thea."

"Yes, Sir." She had read about this, and knew that he would press the plug of ginger into her arse. The natural juices would be in direct contact with her delicate inner tissues. It would feel to be burning, very uncomfortable.

"So, I'll do this slowly so as not to hurt you. I won't use any lube as that reduces the effect of the ginger, but I'll wet the root to make it slide in more easily. I'll need you to remain still, and to co-operate. You'll offer no resistance. Any questions?"

"About the ginger, or the contract, Sir?"

"The ginger. I'll be coming to the contract in due course. Are you ready?"

As I'll ever be. "Yes, Sir."

Tony inserted the tip of his finger first, testing her opening, swirling his digit to loosen the muscle a little. He seemed content to press on though with minimal preparation. Despite his admonition, Thea tensed as the tip of the root entered her.

Her reward was a sharp slap on her bottom. "Open for me. Now." With a conscious effort of will she relaxed her muscle to accept the intrusion. The root slid into place, and her sphincter closed around the grooved section to hold it in place.

"Good. Now, as long as you remain still and don't clench, it won't feel too intense. How are you doing with your reading?"

"Fine, Sir. I think."

"Where have you got to?"

"Here, Sir." She pointed to her place, about a third of the way down the second page.

"Excellent. Continue please."

Thea carried on reading, and was pleased to spot an attempt to extend the period of her secondment to two years. She noted that in the margin, for later.

Tony resumed his assault on her senses by reaching under her to caress her clit. Her body convulsed, sending her arse into a throbbing frenzy.

"Oh God. Please Sir, don't…"

"Carry on reading, Mrs Richmond. And concentrate."

"It hurts. Please."

"I know it hurts. That's the idea. It'll hurt a lot more if I have to spank you for your inattention to the task I've given you." He continued to rub her swollen clit, and Thea wasn't sure if she wanted to orgasm or cry.

"You can't focus on this contract and have an orgasm at the same time. Get your priorities sorted, girl. If you come, I'll spank you."

Right. Crying it is then.

When she reflected back on this scene later Thea had no idea where she dredged up the powers of concentration she managed to find. She focused her vision on the words dancing in front of her eyes and read them. Re-read them. And scribbled in the margin that she would not accept a seventy hour week.

She finished the second sheet and turned that face down too. Tony moved the empty saucer to make room for it on top of the first one. Thea continued, her eyes boring into the third sheet as she battled to contain her rioting senses. This page gave rise to no further notes in the margin, and Thea skim-read it again to make sure. She discarded it onto the read pile and moved on.

The fourth sheet yielded two errors, one arithmetical, the other a spelling mistake. She corrected the first, and made a note against the second.

"What's happening in your head, Mrs Richmond?" Tony's voice was low, he was whispering in her ear. She loved it when he did that during a scene. But he shouldn't be calling her Mrs Richmond, not while she had ginger in her arse and his fingers on her clit.

"I'm confused. Hating this, Sir."

"But you're doing well. You're on page four."

"When I finish reading, will you take the ginger out?"

"Who are you talking to, Mrs Richmond?"

"Don't call me that."

"It's your name. I repeat, who are you talking to?"

"Sir. Sorry, but this feels all wrong."

"Why would it? It's just you and me, and this contract. And the ginger, of course."

"I want to stop."

"Use your safe word then."

Thea shook her head. She was struggling, but not beaten. "No, Sir. I intend to finish."

"Good girl. Let's finish in style then. I'm going to spank you."

"Oh God!"

"Don't pray. Read,"

Thea groaned as he dropped a series of light slaps onto her buttocks. Ordinarily she would have loved this, but she was unable to help herself and was clenching her bottom frantically. The root embedded in her arse caused her to throb like a demon.

"Sir, stop. Please."

"Safe word, or read. I'll stop when you finish the contract." He ramped up the pressure, raining spanks on each of her cheeks, alternating between left and right.

Thea sobbed as she scanned the remaining paragraphs. And narrowly missed a sneaky clause requiring her to greet her new employer on her knees each morning, on his arrival at the office. She was uncertain whether this was a serious requirement or not, in this moment she wouldn't exclude any possibility. She marked the lines with an asterisk and moved on.

"I've finished."

"Good. Hand it to me then. Let me see your notes."

"Sir, the ginger…"

"Your notes, Mrs Richmond."

Thea collected the sheets together, turned them all face up and handed them to Tony.

"Thank you. Please remain where you are until I'm satisfied this task has been completed." He strolled across the room to the sofa where he made himself comfortable to peruse the sheets.

Thea groaned. She removed her glasses, then laid her head on the table. At least now though he had stopped touching her and she could concentrate on her breathing, get her rampant senses under some sort of control. She reflected on the contract, re-running the main terms in her head. Assuming the rogue clauses could be re-drafted, she thought she might quite enjoy working with Tony. He had a sense of humour at least. Even if his approach to negotiations was highly suspect.

"This is a good attempt. You picked up on all but two issues which I would have expected you to query. So, whose work is this? Thea's, or Mrs Richmond's?"

She turned her head to look at him across the room. "It's mine. You saw me do it. I don't understand what you mean."

"This time yesterday I reckon you'd have had no trouble separating the two. Are we perhaps managing to blur the edges a little?"

"I… maybe. I suppose so. But only because you gave me no choice."

"Of course you had a choice. You always do. You could have used your safe word. At one point I thought you might."

"I wanted to please you."

He glanced at her. "You have. You always do, Thea. You delight me."

She was speechless, unsure whether to remain still or dance around the dining table. In view of the ginger still embedded in her arse she opted to stay where she was.

"Thank you, Sir. That means a lot to me."

Tony stood and came back to stand beside her. He dropped the contract on the table. "I think this ginger has done its work now. Hold still."

He had no need to ask twice. Thea held her breath while Tony drew the vile root from her rear hole, then straightened slowly.

"It'll take a few minutes to stop throbbing but you'll be fine soon. Pick up the contract and come here. You'll need your glasses too."

Thea followed him across the room to the sofa. He sat and gestured for her to clamber into his lap. She snuggled into his chest, wriggling in an attempt to gain the friction she needed with a growing desperation. Her bum might be less irritated now, on that point he was correct. But her clit felt to be on fire.

"You seem agitated, Thea. Are you alright?"

"I need to come, Sir. May I…?"

"You may. Would you like me to hold your glasses for you?"

Thea handed him the spectacles, then leaned back to rest her body against the leather-covered cushions, her legs still draped across his lap. She wriggled backwards to give herself more space, then spread her legs wide. Using the fingers of her left hand she parted the lips framing her clit, then she reached down with her right hand. She rubbed the swollen nub she had exposed, slowly at first, then gathering strength as her arousal spiked. She was conscious of his gaze, watching her pleasure herself. She relished it. Despite her desire to orgasm, she slowed her stroking to draw out this moment. Tony said nothing. He leaned back against the sofa, his eyes darkening. Thea looked up at him, smiled, then arched her back. She let out a small cry as her climax overwhelmed her. Shudders wracked her body as waves of accumulated lust pulsed through her, the discharge of the pent up tension she had somehow managed to suppress during the scene. The climax felt to go on for ever, though in reality she supposed it was just a few moments. After, she lay still, limp, her thighs still spread wide.

"Do you feel better now?"

"A little, Sir."

"Are you ready to continue?"

"I'd like you to fuck me, Sir."

"Ah."

"Sir, please…"

"Oh Thea, you do beg so prettily. And I find it hard to refuse you anything when you entertain me so well."

He stood and loosened his jeans, releasing his erection. Thea was delighted to note he seemed to be in a state of some arousal himself. She watched as he produced a condom from the front pocket of his jeans and snapped the foil with his teeth. Moments later, sheathed, he twirled his index finger to indicate she should turn around on the couch. Thea started to move onto all fours.

"No, on your back. Just shift your bum over to the edge."

Thea obeyed, as Tony knelt in front of the couch. He placed his hands on her knees to push them up towards her chest, and outwards, opening her to him. He leaned forward, and with one swift thrust was inside her.

"Oh God. Oh Sir, Sir…"

"Holy fuck, Thea. So tight, every time."

"Harder Sir. Faster."

Tony's response was to draw his hips back, then drive forward again, filling her completely. Thea let out a squeal, clenching around him. She gripped his shoulders, clinging on as her inner muscles convulsed around his cock. A second orgasm was erupting, deep in her core. She considered for perhaps a millisecond the possibility of somehow fighting off her climax, drawing this delight out for longer, but another deep, sharp thrust put a stop to that fantasy.

"Don't hold back, girl. I want you to come. Often, and hard. Now."

Tony's voice was a low growl. He continued to pound into her, his thrusts powerful, demanding, almost savage in their intensity. Thea relinquished any pretence at control as her body arched and convulsed, her second orgasm just moments away.

As her shudders subsided, Tony slowed his thrusts. His strokes now were long and leisurely, a sensual caress, stretching her, the friction rippling against her inner walls. He leaned over to brush his lips across her mouth. Thea parted her lips and his tongue entered, exploring her. He licked, tasted. Their tongues twisted together in an erotic, sensual dance. Thea sucked on his, moving her hands up to tunnel her fingers through his hair. She rarely got to touch him during their scenes, this was a rare treat and she loved the intimacy.

"Christ, girl, you feel so good. So fucking hot."
Thea squeezed around him, lifting her hips. She locked her ankles behind his waist and dug her heels in, drawing him close, then closer still. She had intended to concentrate on his pleasure for a while, but in moments her body tightened again, readying for another climax. She knew better than to fight it now as every sensation, every tingle, every pulsating quiver seemed to coalesce in her pussy. She moaned her delight as her orgasm swept her along, this time to be joined by Tony. His cock lurched inside her and he drove deep one last time, holding the position. His face was buried in her hair as he let out a muffled oath, then went still.
Neither spoke for several minutes. Thea's breath came in short pants, her heart beating a rapid fire tempo inside her chest. Tony was the first to recover. He lifted his weight from her, separated their bodies, and disposed of the condom. Standing, he adjusted his clothing. Thea wondered, not for the first time, how he could create such intensity of sensation for her, controlling her responses, consuming her entirely, whilst seeming not to break a sweat himself. She supposed it was a Dom thing, and thanked God for it.
"Can we deal with this contract now, do you think?" His tone was dry as he picked up the stray sheets of paper now scattered across the floor. He handed the reassembled document to her, then lifted her bodily from the sofa. He sat down and arranged her in his lap, tucking her head beneath his chin. "Where are your glasses, Mrs Richmond?"
"I'm not sure, Sir. Oh, there…" She pointed to the spectacles half-rammed down the space between the cushion and the back of the sofa. Tony helped her to retrieve them and she perched them on her nose.
"Right, let's hear your comments then?"
Ten minutes later the errant clauses had been re-drafted, errors corrected. Tony nuzzled the top of Thea's head. "Would you feel confident about signing this now?"
"I think so, Sir. Yes."
"Good. Even so, I expect you'd prefer to leave the formalities until your first day in the office."

"Maybe. There's still one thing puzzling me though. I have a question, about why you want me to work for you."
"Oh? What's your question, Thea?"
"You must have discovered something amiss, something that makes you suspicious. What is it?"
He paused, considering. "Stephen said you were smart, and I can see nothing much will get past you. You're right. There are a couple of things really. We've had a mauling at an industrial tribunal. A costly one at that, both financially and in terms of our reputation. Dart Logistics needs a serious overhaul to get our staffing systems up to scratch. I'm not saying we haven't got good people, but we don't manage them very well."
"Right. And what else? You said a couple of things."
"Finance. Our year-end figures seem inconsistent with predictions earlier in the year. It was the same last year. It could be just down to poor forecasting, but I have a feeling there's more to it. I need someone to audit our accounts for the last couple of years and tell me what's going on."
"If you know already where the problems are, why do you need me? Why not just put your house in order yourself?"
"Mrs Richmond, do you ride a bicycle?"
"I beg your pardon?"
"A bicycle, Mrs Richmond. Do you own one?"
"No, of course not."
"You should try it. Excellent cardio-vascular exercise, although I confess I do rather enjoy giving you a workout myself." He paused to caress her breast, his palm massaging the soft mound before he took her nipple between his finger and thumb and rolled it gently. Thea gasped and arched her back, loving his touch. "Thank you, Sir. You are very good for my heart rate. I don't believe I'll be purchasing a bicycle any time soon. I did have a bike as a child though."
"I see. Did you fall off it much? Crash it into trees, that sort of thing?" Tony continued to squeeze and stroke her swelling nipple and Thea found her concentration wandering once more. A firm pinch brought her back into focus.
"From time to time. I survived."

"I'll bet you were good at pedalling."

"Yes. I suppose. I was fast."

"I can imagine that, your little legs pumping. But without your hands on the handlebars and your eyes looking where you were going, you'd have gone round in circles. Crashed. Probably ended up in the canal or worse. Then where would your faultless, fast pedalling have got you? It would be better not to pedal at all than to do it without direction, without a sense of where you're going. Do you agree?"

"Yes, I suppose so. But neither can you just sit there pointing your front wheel at things. You need to make it go."

"Exactly. I run my company. I have my hands on the handlebars and I'm looking ahead. I keep Dart Logistics out of the canal, Mrs Richmond. But I rely on others, you, to do most of the pedalling. You could say I'm a leader, a figurehead. You though, you're a manager. And a bloody good one. It's because of good managers that businesses run well. I can steer, but you do exemplary pedalling, Mrs Richmond, and that's why I need you. We're a team. Or we will be."

"I couldn't do what you do. Take charge."

"I don't want you to, not here in my home, or in the dungeon. And not at work either. But I do need your technical skills, your understanding of systems and such like. I'm not good at that stuff. So I need someone on my team who is. That's you, Thea."

His persistent manipulation of her pebbled nub had ceased. Thea turned in his arms to face him, kneeling in his lap.

"But, you seem so confident. Always. You don't need me. You don't need anyone."

"That's where you're wrong, Mrs Richmond. I do need you. So, where do you think we should start?"

"You keep on about me working for you, and maybe you're right, perhaps it could work. But it's hard. Terrifying in fact. I can't just dump the habits of a lifetime..."

"Do you need to revisit your contract, Mrs Richmond? I believe I may still have some ginger in the fridge."

"No! I don't mean that. You made your point and I'm not arguing with you. I just need to take this slower. If you'll allow that. Please."

"I need you on the case, Thea. Now."

"I know, but…"

"How about if you work remotely? At least at first?"

"What? How do you mean?"

"I mean, all my systems at Dart are online. You could log in from anywhere, here for example, and start by overhauling them."

Thea stared at him, struck not for the first time at his ingenuity and his inventive, flexible approach. In her business life as much as in her kink he was able to anticipate and overcome her issues, her hangups. He made it safe for her. Why had she ever doubted she could work with him as well as play?

She nodded, slowly. "Yes, that could work. I'd be happy doing that for you."

"Excellent. So, I'll ask you again. Where would you like to start?"

"Start? I'm not sure I…"

"Please try to keep up, Mrs Richmond. I mean, now that we've sorted out the methodology, where are you going to begin your overhaul of Dart Logistics?"

Thea's head cleared, the ground once more solidifying beneath her. For the first time in days, ever since she'd walked into his office to discover her worlds colliding before her eyes, she felt in charge, certain.

"Oh, finance. Definitely. If the money's not under control, nothing is. And problems with the accounting system can be pretty fatal if not put right, but they are usually easy to rectify. We get that solid, then look at the rest."

"Okay. When can you start?"

"Tomorrow."

"It's Sunday tomorrow."

"Yes, so no one else will be around. I'll have a clear run at it, no distractions. Can you let me into your office in the morning?"

"I could, if necessary. But we agreed you can access our networks from here."

"I'd like to make an early start then. If that's alright with you."

"It sounds very sensible. Perhaps we should get an early night…"

Chapter six

"We have—eggs, two rashers of bacon, some cereals, and half an onion." Tony turned to Thea, the fridge door still standing open. "I could rustle up an omelette I suppose."

"Sounds fine. Do you want me to make it?"

"No. I want you to sit there, drink your tea, and tell me what you make of those mid-year accounts. You wanted an early start, remember."

"Okay." Thea perched her glasses back on her nose and turned her attention back to the laptop open in front of her. She clicked the mouse a couple of times, and made notes on a sheet of paper next to her.

Tony watched, loving her quiet, studious efficiency. Having abdicated responsibility for their breakfast, Thea's concentration on the matter in hand was total. He admired her single-mindedness, particularly as this was a quality he'd never cultivated for himself. It wasn't that he didn't value clarity and focus, but for Tony the real fascination always lay on the far horizon, the allure of possibility and opportunity, of what ifs.

Ten minutes later he slid a plate onto the table beside her. Thea acknowledged it with a slight nod, her gaze never leaving the screen. Tony took his seat opposite and contented himself with sipping his coffee and watching his newest member of staff at work. She hadn't formally accepted his job offer yet, but she would.

It was just over an hour later when she lifted her solemn, serious gaze to his. "I think you have a thief in your accounts section. Maybe more than one."

"What!" He'd known there was an issue, but had convinced himself it was one of cock-up not conspiracy. "Why? What have you seen?"

"Some entries in your spreadsheets are out of sync. By which I mean, entered much later than others relating to the same transactions. I've been tracking the changes, and finding amendments which seem to indicate that clients' accounts are in debit, when earlier records had shown those same accounts to be up to date or even in credit. That's consistent with someone removing funds, then amending records to conceal the discrepancy.

It's been going on for quite a long time too, at least a couple of years."

"So, who...?"

"The culprits will be easy to identify. I'll see to that for you in due course. For now, our priority is to seize and seal all evidence. That means closing down your entire network so that only you and I can access any records. If I get started now I can eliminate those parts of your system that aren't affected and put those back on line. By Monday morning Dart Logistics will be functional again, apart from the finance section I imagine. You need to suspend all your finance team on full pay until my investigation is complete. Two days, I'd estimate, though the police may extend that."

"Shit. Are you sure? And are you saying it's a police matter?"

She peered at him over her rimless glasses. "Financial records have been tampered with. I'm guessing at the most likely reason for that but I suspect fraud, and my recommendation is that you authorise me to undertake an immediate forensic audit. And yes, if when I've completed that audit we believe a theft has taken place then that would suggest involving the police. Or do you prefer to deal with it in another way?"

He regarded her, then nodded. "Let's get to the bottom of what's happened first, then decide what action to take. Do the audit. What will you need?"

"Some clothes. I came here without much last night if you recall. There's a limit to how much more I can actually achieve via remote access because I need access to some hard copy documents too—invoices and such like—to check against spreadsheets. But it's Sunday so I could go into your premises and get started. If you could run me back to my flat, then let me into your offices and leave me to it..."

Tony grinned. She was wearing an old T shirt of his, and was without doubt the sexiest auditor he'd ever seen. But she was right. She needed her own stuff.

"Okay. I'll drive you home. You can change, get anything else you'll need, and we'll go to Dart. The warehouse will be open, that part of the operation is twenty four seven. And security of course..."

She shook her head. "Your security team are suspects the same as anyone else. You need them out of the picture too, until my audit is complete. Can I suggest you ask Stephen for a couple of his men, just to manage the building, and give your team a couple of days off too? Full pay, obviously."

"Obviously. Right. You can phone Stephen from the car. Let's get moving."

*****

Tony felt redundant. Thea had hardly lifted her gaze from first one terminal, then the next for the last five hours. She was working her way through all his systems, jotting down notes, checking input data against invoices, even requesting that cheques be recalled from their bank.

"I think that's how the money was syphoned off. Online transactions are easily tracked, the payee electronically recorded. Cheques are easier to fudge. A number, an ambiguous payee name. That's how I'd do it."

"You?"

"Yes, me. If you want to work out how a thief has managed to steal from you the best place to start is to try to work out how you'd have done it. You know your system's weaknesses, where would you head for? And be sure, if your financial controls are not watertight, if there's a way to defraud your company someone, at some time, will do it. Dart isn't secure. It will be, soon. But right now... no."

Tony gave her a wry smile as he picked up the phone to call his head of finance. Thea could deal with his systems and root out his bad apples. He'd deal with the suspensions.

*****

"Mr diMarco, there's a David Lister at the front desk. I explained that the company is closed but he insists."

"Right. I'll come down." Tony replaced the phone when his temporary security manager, seconded to Dart by a somewhat startled Stephen Kershaw, hung up. He glanced at Thea. "My

Finance Director's arrived. I've been expecting him. He took the news of his suspension hard."

"You can't let him in."

"Got that. Do you want a sandwich or anything, while I'm down there? I think there's a Polish deli open on Sundays."

"Chicken salad please. No mayo."

Dismissed, Tony left her to continue her investigations while he went down to placate his irate corporate accountant.

Another two hours passed. And another two. Thea was still hard at it. Tony had fielded dozens of calls from anxious employees as news of the suspensions circulated, but now the flow had dried up. It was just the two of them. Well, more accurately, Thea, and him keeping her supplied with tea. She was a demon with the IT, over-riding passwords, isolating first one part of his network then another, narrowing down the area they had to search. By ten thirty that evening he was exhausted, but she still looked to be going strong.

"When do you want to pack it in for the night?"

"When I'm finished."

"We'll come back tomorrow. Look at it fresh."

"I don't want to look at it fresh. I have it now. Almost. Another few hours…"

"You mean you want to work through the night?"

"Yes. That's best. That way nothing gets lost. Or forgotten. No chance of anyone tampering."

"The office is locked up, the systems offline."

"A clever thief might be able to get in remotely. And by now they all know we're onto something. The thief must be panicking. Really, I'd prefer to stay here and see this through. You don't have to though."

Tony leaned back in his chair and placed his feet on his desk. "If you're staying, so am I. Shall I order up a pizza?"

Thea just smiled, nodded, and returned to her work.

*****

"I'm done. We can go home now?" Thea tapped Tony on the shoulder not sure of the protocols in awakening a sleeping Dom. Especially one who has been made to stay at his office all night while she combed through pretty much every file in his system. He'd been sweet tempered about it, keeping her supplied with junk food and occasionally massaging her neck for her. But he'd wanted to go home, and she had refused. That would have consequences, and right now she was bone tired. She hoped he'd let her sleep all day and take up any outstanding issues later. Much later. "Sir? Tony? I've finished."

"What? All of it?" He opened one eye to peer up at her.

"Yes. All of it. I'm pretty certain I know what's been happening, and I have the evidence you'll need to confront the staff responsible. As I feared, it's probably a matter for the police though rather than for your disciplinary procedures. I have a file for them."

"A... you have a file for the police?"

"Yes. Fraud is a criminal offence. Your Mr Lister has some questions to answer and so do Mrs Benson in purchasing, and Mrs Reece in dispatch. It's all in here." She tapped the envelope file where she had stored the originals of the documents the police would find of most interest. "I expect they'll want to send their own IT specialists in to crawl all over your systems. It's all set up ready for them."

"Who did you say? David Lister, and...?"

"Mrs Benson, she's been generating ghost purchase orders, and as far as I can make out pocketing the associated payments. She had help from Shirley Reece in your dispatch team. They're cousins. David Lister knew about it and they gave him a cut to turn a blind eye. It's been going on for nearly three years, ever since Mrs Benson started here. It's all in there." Thea tapped the file she'd placed on his desk. "I suggest we go back to your house. Or if you want you can drop me at home. I need to get some sleep. And you can read through the file before we hand it over to the police."

"What time is it?"

"Twenty to seven."

"Shit. And you've been working all night. You look ready to drop."

"I *am* tired. I just don't like leaving a job like that, once I've got into it. Thank you for letting me stay. And for waiting."

Tony got to his feet, stretching. "You're the hero of the hour, Mrs Richmond. It was the least I could do. Come on. Home, bed, sleep.

Before you fall over. And thank you." He kissed her on the mouth, then took her hand to tow her out of his office. He grabbed the file from his desk as he passed.

In the foyer he paused to exchange a few words with the temporary security guard he'd borrowed from Kershaw's. He was frowning as they left the building.

"David Lister was back here late last night, after he spoke to me. He became abusive, and only left when he was threatened with the police. We'll have trouble from him I reckon."

"He'll be scared. But it's already too late for him to do anything to cover his tracks. That's why we needed to seal the evidence as soon as I suspected, and prevent anyone accessing it. Standard forensic accountancy procedure and it means I can stand up in court and swear to the accuracy of the data we've supplied."

"Will it come to that, do you think?"

"Well, we have enough to justify dismissal, but there's always the chance one or more of them might decide to challenge us. Better to have the police investigation to fall back on. And it's good for encouraging the others. You know, show them you won't tolerate thieves."

"You're right, but still it leaves an unpleasant taste." He held the door open for her and they exited into the car park, still grey in the early morning light.

"Mr diMarco! Tony. Do you have a moment?"

"Oh fuck, I thought we'd got rid of him. Thea, this is David Lister." Tony paused and nodded at the middle aged, slightly dishevelled man barrelling towards them. A sleek BMW was parked in the corner of the parking area, its driver's door swinging open where its occupant had leapt out to confront the pair now leaving the building.

"Good morning, David. Have you been here all night?"

"I wanted to talk to you. Those idiots wouldn't let me in. I told them I work here, I'm in charge of finance. You'll need me to help sort this mess out."

"Thank you, but we have it under control. Now if you'll excuse us..."

"But you owe me some sort of explanation. I've worked here for years, I know these systems better than anyone. If there was anything amiss I'd be the first to spot it."

Tony made to sidestep him. "Thank you, Mr Lister. We'll be in touch in the next few days."

"We? Who's we? And who's this? What's she doing here?" He jabbed a finger in Thea's direction. She stepped back, out of his reach.

Tony placed himself between Thea and his disgruntled soon-to-be ex-employee. "May I introduce Mrs Richmond? She recently joined my team as Dart Logistics' new Corporate Services Director."

"Why do we need her? And why wasn't I involved in making the new appointment? It's my job, anything to do with finance. You know that." David Lister's voice had risen, he was almost shouting at Tony now. Thea was relieved to spot the security guard exiting the building.

Tony appeared unfazed. "I'll let you know if we need anything from you, David. Now if you'll excuse me...." He turned to the guard who had reached them. "Ah, yes. Mr Lister was just leaving. Could you make sure he gets away safely please? Oh, and David, if we could just have your electric key to the car park back, please…?"

"What? Why? I'll be needing it."

"In which case it will be returned to you in due course. Could you hand it over to security please, or if it's easier for you we'll just deactivate it."

Silenced at last, David Lister glared at his boss. Tony seemed to consider this a good opportunity to make their exit, and placed his hand on Thea's elbow to direct her towards the practical Ford parked in the bay marked CEO. Thea reflected that Tony must pay excellent salaries if his staff could drive around in BMWs. Perhaps she should look again at that contract.

*****

Thea opened her eyes and peered at the window opposite where she lay in Tony's bed. Sunlight streamed through the curtains throwing golden pools across the dark blue carpet in the bedroom. She rolled over, and winced as her bladder gave her an insistent prod. She needed to get up. She squinted at the small clock on the bedside table. Three fifteen.

Three fifteen! Shit! She'd been asleep nearly all day. She needed to get up, she had work to do, an investigation to finish. And where the Hell was Tony anyway?

She shot out of bed and rushed across the room to the en suite loo. Her comfort restored, she charged back into the bedroom and started to throw on her clothes. Was her car still outside? She went to the window to check. Yes. Where were her keys? How long would it take to get to Dart's offices?

Her phone buzzed in the pocket of her jeans as she jogged downstairs. She pulled it out. Caller ID told her Tony was on the line.

She answered it, breathless. "Hi. I overslept, sorry. Where are you?"

"At the office. You were spark out so I left you to get some rest."

"You should have woken me. Or sent me an alarm call. Something. I'm just on my way."

"Well stop being on your way. Everything's under control here. You've earned a day off."

"I can't take a day off. I haven't started work yet."

"Oh. So who was it who turned in a twenty four hour shift yesterday then? It looked like you. Seriously, Thea, we're fine. The police want to interview you, but I told them you'd be in tomorrow and they'll come back then. They took your file. They seemed to think we could probably reinstate the finance team, with the obvious three exceptions. Would you agree?"

"Yes, if the police are happy I think that'd be fine. I collected all the evidence they're likely to need and it's important for you to get your company back to normal as soon as possible. You'll need to put someone in charge of finance temporarily."

"I was thinking I'd go to an agency."

"Can I suggest Mrs Metcalfe? She's been David Lister's assistant for two years so she knows the job. And there's no evidence linking her to his scam."

Tony was silent for a few moments. Thea suspected he was trying to place the name. "She's rather young…"

"Twenty four. She's bright, and she's honest…"

"Well that counts for something I suppose."

"I think so. It's your choice, but from what I've seen in her personnel file I'm happy to recommend her. And she could start immediately."
Thea made her way into the kitchen. She wedged the phone between her shoulder and her ear as she clicked the switch on the kettle and hunted up a cup and the caddy containing Earl Grey teabags. A few seconds later the gentle hiss of soon to be boiling water lent its own comforting tone to the silent room. Still, she couldn't entirely reconcile herself to not appearing at the office at all that day. It would be pleasant though to take her tea back upstairs, snuggle up in Tony's king size bed, maybe have a shower later…
"Okay. You're my corporate services director, I guess it's your call. Mrs Metcalfe it is then. Will you talk to her tomorrow? I suppose we'll have to brief her on what's been going on."
"I'll handle that if you're happy to leave it with me. I'm confident about the outcome, but these are still just allegations until the police have conducted their enquiries so we need to be careful what we actually say."
"Fine. Understood. I'll get started phoning round to tell the rest of the team to come back in. And you Mrs Richmond, can just chill out, watch some daytime TV. Relax."
Thea smiled as she dropped her teabag into the cup and poured the hot water over with her free hand. A day off was starting to sound particularly attractive, though she would pass on the daytime television. "Maybe I'll take a bath. When will you be home?"
"Not late, Around sevenish I expect. Will you still be there?"
"Do you want me to be? I could go home…"
"I want you to be."
Something squeezed and warmed, low down in her belly. Thea's pussy moistened.
"Should I cook? I could probably find something…"
"I'll bring a takeaway."
"Okay. Shall I wait for you in the dining room?"
"Now there's an attractive thought. I'll bring something we can re-heat."

Chapter seven

Would she take the hint? He hoped so. He could give her explicit instructions, she would obey him, no question. Given the twist their relationship had taken he probably needed to spell out his expectations in more detail, and he would. Soon. Still, it would be interesting to see how she interpreted their conversation this afternoon.

She'd be in the dining room when he arrived he was sure of that. But would she be perched on a chair, fully dressed, the table laid for their meal? Or would he find her kneeling, naked, her collar to hand ready for him to fasten it around her neck?

His cock swelled and hardened in his trousers at the thought. He shifted in the driver's seat, trying to make himself more comfortable. He was still thirty minutes from home.

It had been an eventful day. He'd grabbed a couple of hours sleep when he and Thea first got back to his house, but as he'd been dozing most of the previous night while she worked he wasn't that tired. He got up around mid-morning. Thea was in a deep sleep, but still he crept around the bedroom so as not to wake her, and he left for the office.

He'd picked up a take-out coffee on the way, and arrived at his office just before lunchtime, to find the staff wandering around bemused. He couldn't blame them really. The place was rife with gossip and rumours, most of which seemed to arrive at the conclusion the firm was about to close and they'd all be out of a job. He'd called an immediate staff meeting in the canteen. It was standing room only. He explained that there had been some accounting and admin irregularities, but that everything was now under control and they should all continue their duties as normal. The absence of the entire finance section did not go unnoticed, but he opted to make no reference to that. No one else saw fit to point it out either, with one exception.

"Come on. Spill. What's going on?" Isabel had followed him back from the canteen and into his office. She plonked herself in the chair across from his desk and crossed her legs. She was going nowhere without an explanation.

Tony had regarded his most trusted employee, the assistant who had mopped up his messes for the last ten years and whose loyalty was not in doubt. "Fraud. It's a police matter. Or it will be. I'm about to call them in."

"Shit! What? But how? Who…?" He'd allowed himself a quiet smirk. Isabel was rarely rattled, let alone lost for words. She hadn't seen that coming though.

Not that he'd had any notion either. But for Thea this bunch of thieves would have carried on making a fool of him for a while yet. He'd have cottoned to it eventually, but they'd have got away with a lot more of his cash before he did. As it was, he reckoned Thea's estimate of around a hundred and twenty thousand pounds between them, over two to three years, was conservative. In his experience thieves were greedy people. Once they got their little scam set up, they'd have milked it for all they could get. He had much to thank her for. He would see to that. Later.

"Tony, what's been happening?" Isabel had leaned forward in her chair, demanding answers. Tony sighed. Where to start?

"Remember Mrs Richmond? The woman I wanted to headhunt from Kershaw's?"

Isabel had nodded. "The one you managed to scare off?" There was a derisory note in his PA's tone. She had been less than impressed on first meeting Thea. Tony could understand why, but it had rankled even so.

"That was a misunderstanding, and entirely my fault. I ran into Mrs Richmond over the weekend. We talked, and I managed to convince her to give us—me—another chance." It was sort of the truth. Near enough. As near as he was going.

"Right, And…"

"And I briefed her on the problem areas, as I saw them. Finance and human resources. She agreed to have an initial look at our financial management processes and something caught her eye. She spotted a serious fraud going on. It involves Janet Benson and Shirley Reece, and David Lister."

"But when? When did Mrs Richmond do all this?"

"Yesterday, mostly. We were here all day, and all night."

"You were here all last night? Working? Why didn't you call me? I'd have come in."

Why indeed? The truth was, it had never occurred to him but he didn't think his loyal PA for the last ten years, his right-hand woman, needed to hear that.

"I know you would. But there was no need. We just went through everything—well, Mrs Richmond did—and isolated the three culprits."

"I see." She offered him a smile, but it had a brittle quality about it. Tony resolved not to exclude her again. He needed Thea's special skills to set his ailing company in order, but Isabel was invaluable too. She continued, her expression softening to a more thoughtful look. "I know Mr Lister of course, but the other two…"

"Janet works in Purchasing, Shirley in Dispatch. Or they did. They're suspended right now and likely to stay that way. I need to alert the police and pass on Mrs Richmond's findings. Do you want to sit in on that?" His last question had been a concession to Isabel's wounded pride and a deliberate, if belated, attempt to involve her.

"Too right I bloody do. Christ, I can't believe this. Where's Mrs Richmond now? Shouldn't she be here? With the police, I mean…?"

"She was up all night checking our systems and working out what had been going on. She's at home. In bed."

"She must be exhausted. I'll give her a ring later, see if she's alright. I think I have her home number in a file somewhere."

Tony had offered a tactful cough. No point in trying to explain to his PA why the formidable Mrs Richmond was at his home, asleep in his bed and not her own. Maybe another time.

"Can you find me a number for the fraud squad, please? I want to get this ball rolling. The sooner we report it and hand over this file, the sooner I can get what's left of my finance team back to work."

"Are you sure we need to involve the police? Surely we could deal with this in house."

"That's not what Mrs Richmond is advising, and this is her area of expertise."

"I see. Well if that's what Mrs Richmond says…" She shook her head in apparent disbelief. "David Lister—shit. By the way, he's tried four times so far this morning to call you. Should I put him through next time?"

"No. He's been hanging around all weekend, ever since I phoned him to say his department was being investigated. He was even waiting for us when we left here at seven o'clock this morning. He was pretty agitated. I've said all I'm going to as far as he's concerned. He can discuss it with the police."

"Right. Talking of which, I'll get you that number."

Three hours later Tony leaned back in his chair and stretched. Christ, what a day. The police had left, Thea's file tucked under the inspector's arm. Inspector Collywood seemed impressed though, and did at least understand the data she had printed off. So did Tony, after a fashion, but the fine detail escaped him as it always did. He lacked the patience to drill down into it, preferring to rely on Thea and now the police specialist fraud investigators. They intended to interview Thea, and following that they would talk to the three suspects. Inspector Collywood was content to leave his further enquiries until the following day, observing that no one would be going anywhere, and he wanted to study the details in more depth himself first.

Tony had dragged his phone from his pocket and found Thea on speed dial.

That had been a few hours ago. After talking to her and convincing her to take the rest of the day off he'd spent the rest of the afternoon on the phone to his finance staff, asking them to return to work the next morning. Just before five o'clock he took a call from Shirley Reece who had no doubt been alerted by the finance grapevine that most of her colleagues had been reinstated. She apologised, said she had been out shopping and must have missed his call earlier, and asked what time she should come in the next morning.

"That's quite alright, Mrs Reece. Thank you for calling. But we won't be requiring you back at work tomorrow."

"Oh. When then?"

"We'll be in touch soon."

"Am I still being paid? I want my money. It's not my fault. None of this is my doing."

"None of what. Mrs Reece?"

"This. Whatever. I don't know. But there must be something up, else you'd not be carrying on like this. Just don't be trying to pin it on me, that's all."

"I can confirm that you are still on full pay, Mrs Reece. And we'll be in touch with you in the coming days. Goodbye."

He replaced the receiver. Such remaining doubts as he might have been clinging to—and those were slender enough—now dissolved. In his experience people never denied something they had not been accused of, unless they'd done it. Shirley Reece was in a lot of bother.

And he had a lovely submissive waiting for him at home, but first he had a couple of errands to see to on the way there.

Tony pulled up in his driveway alongside Thea's car. He glanced up at the windows but saw no face watching for him. A good sign. The dining room was on the other side of the house. He picked up the carrier bag containing a takeaway selection of Chinese dishes and mounted the steps up to the front door to let himself in.

Silence. He put his briefcase down on the floor in the hall and sauntered along the polished wood floor. The dining room door was closed, but he knew she was there as surely as if the solid ash panel was made of glass. He carried on along the hallway to the kitchen where he deposited his carrier bag. His footsteps echoed in the quiet hallway as he strode back to the dining room. He turned the handle and pushed the door open.

Thea knelt on the floor, her back to him. She was naked, her slender back ramrod straight. Even so, her posture looked relaxed, practised. She was at ease in and with herself, and this pleased him. He didn't speak, but of course she was aware of his presence. He saw that in the slight tilt of her chin, the almost imperceptible clench of her fingers as they rested on her thighs.

He walked past her and sat on the sofa. Her head was bowed but he knew she watched him, her eyes following him as he moved. He removed his suit jacket and draped it across the seat next to him, then he loosened his tie. His cuffs were next. He unfastened them and rolled back his shirt sleeves, then he leaned back.

"Do you feel rested now, Thea?"

"Yes, Sir. Very. I had a bath too. I feel very pampered."

"You earned it. So, Thea, how would you like to spend the evening?"

"With you, Sir."

"Yet you offered to return to your apartment. Why?"

"You said you like to live alone, Sir. I don't want to crowd you, if you need your space."

"I have plenty of space here, whether you're in the house or not."

"Yes, Sir. I can see that."

"So, just to make sure there's no misunderstanding between us on this matter, you're welcome to stay here as often as you like. You can sleep here every night if you want to."

"In your bed, Sir."

"Of course."

"What about my apartment?"

"Keep it. Sub-let it if you want. Or you might want to sleep there sometimes too. I'm not the only one who said they like to live alone."

"Thank you, Sir."

"Why are you thanking me, Thea?"

"For being nice, Sir."

Tony chuckled. "I wonder if you'll still feel like thanking me when I have you tied to my bed and you're begging me to let you come."

"There's only one way to find out, Sir."

*****

Thea stretched, tugging at the ropes that held her immobile. She lay spread eagled across the mattress, her wrists tied to the headboard and her ankles secured to the foot of the bed. Her hips were raised. A pile of several pillows shoved under her bottom arched her back, rendering her body accessible for whatever her Dom might choose to do to her. She was blindfolded too, her remaining senses acutely attuned to whatever stimulation might be served up. She wasn't gagged, but he had instructed her to remain silent unless asked a direct question, or unless she wanted to safe word. She would not be doing that. He might as well have stopped her mouth.

The room was deathly quiet but for the faint tick of a clock, but she knew she was not alone. Tony was here.

She parted her lips, drawing her tongue across the lower one. Cool air whispered over her breasts, the first, the only indication that he was about to…

"Oh, aah." Despite Tony's instructions she couldn't contain a moan as the fronds of the soft suede flogger trailed across her shoulders then down the centre of her torso to her belly. As suddenly as they arrived, they were gone. She thrust her hips further up, seeking, blindly questing. The air fluttered again, and the strands drifted across her breasts this time, curling lovingly around her swollen nipples. The movement was slow, unhurried, tracing a leisurely path over her sensitive skin.

"Tony. Sir. Oh God…"

"Do you like this, Thea?"

"Yes. More, please."

"More then, but you must remain silent. If you don't, this will become a lot less pleasant for you. Do you understand me?"

Thea nodded, determined not to give him any cause to limit her pleasure tonight.

Tony flicked her right nipple with the flogger, the sudden bite of pleasure/pain gone almost before it was there. He trailed and teased some more, caressing her straining body with the soft, light implement. Thea writhed on the mattress, straining towards him, desperate to savour every brush and stroke.

He moved lower, dragging the suede over her abdomen, his strokes feather-light and barely there. Another flick and the strands snapped against her taut skin causing her to gasp. He repeated the action, harder now, definitely looking to cause pain rather than pleasure. Thea moaned again, gyrating her hips in a wordless appeal.

"Ah, you want me to flog your pussy? You are such a slut, Thea."

"Your slut, Master." She bit her lip, too late remembering his instruction. Would he take issue with her lapse?

"Mine." Seemingly not. This time.

The bed dipped beside her as he settled his weight on it, then Thea shrieked as the flogger snaked across the lips of her pussy.
She'd known what he would do, yet still the shock took her breath away. It hurt, beautifully. The pain was a sweet, tantalising dance of wildfire across her throbbing cunt. Tony waited for a few moments, and Thea fought to control the impulse to squeeze her legs together. Not that she could move, Tony's skill with ropes saw to that. She lay still, her body tensed, waiting for the next stroke.
It didn't come. The bed shifted again, and she knew he was no longer sharing it with her. She strained her ears, listening for any clue, the slightest sound. She could just detect his footsteps as he moved barefoot around the room.
Her entire body jolted at the next contact, delicate, sharp, teasing the inside of her wrist. The sensation rippled along her arm, past her inner elbow, towards her shoulder.
The pinwheel. He explored her body with it, the sharp spikes scratching the surface of her sensitised skin. She lay still, stiffening as he rolled the wheel across her pebbled nipples, then around her aureole. As if that was not enough, he leaned in to blow on the throbbing peaks, then licked them to make them cooler still. Thea chewed on her lip, almost mad with longing. She wanted his mouth, his tongue, his teeth, but he seemed inclined to offer nothing but the merest brush of his fingers, and the delicate prickle of the pinwheel. She might have begged him, pleaded with him for the friction she craved. But that would be useless. Worse than useless, it would earn her a punishment for breaking the enforced silence.
Tony traced a pathway from her breasts to her stomach, around her belly button and down to the junction between her thighs. She was wet, dripping, her moisture dampening the sheet beneath her.
"So wet, my slut. You really have no self-control, do you?"
Thea shook her head, convinced that her clit must be swollen to at least ten times its usual size. Would he? Please, please, please...
The wheel continued its inexorable path, tracing the outline of her pussy lips, first one side, then back along the other. He followed the route again, then once more. Thea was dragging in precious oxygen, her head thrown back as her body arched even more, stretched out tight as a bow string.

"Sir, please…"

"Wait. Not yet. I'll tell you when, and you'll come on my command. Not before."

Thea groaned, but knew better than to argue with him on this. Tony would have his way, or he would punish her for setting the pace, for taking matters into her own hands, however helpless she might be. He dominated her, totally, absolutely, and she relished it. This was what she was born for, this was the reason she was on this planet, her existence revolved around these moments. Her reality shrank to just this room, and her stern Dom, as he caressed her straining, needy body, controlled every nerve ending.

Tony used his free hand to part her pussy lips, and he rolled the pinwheel along the delicate inner flesh. The gossamer menace of the sharp spikes scraped her clit, and she shivered, her orgasm hovering just beneath the surface. Her senses were at a breaking point, her consciousness about to shatter. She couldn't control this, was powerless to hold back.

"Sir…" The word was a plea, a strangled, desperate moan. "I can't. No more. No more, please…"

"But you can, my slut. You can do more. You're not ready yet. I'll tell you when it's time."

Behind the blindfold her eyes were screwed up, tight shut. She clenched her fists as her pussy convulsed, her body wracked with shudders as she fought the desperate, losing battle. Tony was relentless, drawing the wheel along her wide open pussy, over the tip of her clit, then around the sides of the throbbing nub until she was near incoherent with lust.

Then he stopped. Just stopped. The wheel was gone, her twitching senses bereft. She lay still; shivering.

The bed dipped again. Tony was beside her, his body stretched out alongside hers once more. His chest was bare, she felt the rasp of the soft hairs which were scattered across his pecs against the delicate skin of her inner arm. He palmed her breast, his touch gentle but firm. He pinched her nipple, the pressure exquisite.

Now, yes. At last. Enough. Almost…

His hand was gone. She thought she might cry. Probably was weeping already.

He shifted again, and she let out a ragged moan as he sank two long fingers into her drenched, drooling pussy. She squeezed, gyrating her hips to force the friction. He let her, didn't order her to stop. She ground against him, seeking the release she now needed more than oxygen.

"Now. Come for me, slut."

The impact was instant. The low, seductive timbre of his voice connected directly to something in her core, and she detonated. His fingers were motionless inside her as she convulsed around them, her body rocking, writhing, contorting against the ropes that bound her as wave after sensual wave crashed through her system. Every muscle, every sinew, every over-stimulated nerve ending spasmed. Her head was spinning, her senses reeling. She was flying, or perhaps plummeting to earth from some dizzying height. And none of it mattered. Nothing mattered to her outside of this all-consuming need her Dom evoked. And satisfied.

Hours, or maybe just moments later, her body went still. She lay, panting, her heart thumping against her breastbone as her world righted itself.

Tony's fingers were gentle as he removed the blindfold to bring her blinking back into the light. She still was not ready to open her eyes though. He released her ankles, then her wrists. Then he pulled her into his arms and held her, shivering against him. He was solid, warm, unshakable. She knew he had her, and she was safe

"Talk to me, Thea."

"Sir? I love you."

"Mmm, good to hear. Not too intense then?"

"Maybe. Definitely. But it was good. And I *do* love you."

"I love you too, my sweet slut. I love your hot, tight pussy, and I adore the way you go wild when you come. I think I may need to fuck you."

"Yes, you might."

"Or perhaps I should spank you, for being such a greedy, slutty little sub."

"Either would be nice, Sir. Or both.

"Roll over then. On all fours."

Thea did as he instructed, lifting her bottom up and planting her knees wide apart. She crossed her arms on the mattress and rested her head on them.

Tony rolled from the bed and went to the wardrobe. He returned carrying a polished wood paddle, quite beautiful. It was solid looking, the shape and size reminiscent of a table tennis bat but she suspected this would be a great deal heavier.

"Sir, I didn't know you had that."

"A recent acquisition. I bought it with you in mind and I suspect it will become one of my favourites. I've been keeping this one for a special occasion. It packs quite a punch I believe."

"I want it, Sir. I want it hard."

"And you shall have it. Hard. Tell me when you've had enough."

Thea nodded, then dropped her forehead back onto her arms.

She lurched forward when the first swat landed, heavy and solid against her left buttock. The bite resounded through her, sinking deep into her flesh.

"Christ, Sir. That *does* sting."

"A few more, I think. To warm you up ready to be fucked."

"Yes. Thank you, Sir."

The next three slaps were delivered in quick succession, and Thea screamed with each one. The paddle was long. It could strike both sides of her bum at once, and her Dom seemed intent on covering her entire arse with its scorching fire. Her pussy was open and exposed, but Tony avoided striking her there. She was glad, though perhaps a little disappointed too. The aftershocks of each spank resonated through her trembling buttocks, and her pussy vibrated with the intensity of it. The next two slaps evoked sharp grunts from her. She was nearing the limit of her endurance, but she hated having to ask her Dom to stop. A couple more would be fine, maybe three or four.

The paddle whistled through the air again and landed full across the back of her right thigh. Thea let out a scream and grasped the duvet in her fist. She was sobbing now, her bottom clenching as she dug deep to ride the pain. Her natural endorphins helped, and would be coursing through her body by the bucket load. She was going to

need a lot more than that to weather the rest of this paddling though.
"Do you want me to stop?"
Thea shook her head.
"Liar."
"Sir?"
"You're at your limit. You can tell me that. You know you can."
"I'm not, I…"
He laid the paddle on the bed beside her. Thea sighed and reached for his hand, only now succumbing to the wave of relief, now that the paddling was over.
"Why didn't you say?"
"No need. You always know."
"One day I might not. I'm not psychic. What if I didn't notice and pushed you past your limit? You should protect yourself."
"If you were a Dom who didn't take notice I would never have agreed to wear your collar. I wouldn't have scened with you all these months."
"Fair point I suppose. Even so, one day I intend to punish you for this lax habit of yours. Not today though. Today I'm too pleased with you to want to correct your behaviour. But be warned, Mrs Richmond…"
"Why do you keep calling me that?"
"It's your name. One of them, anyway. So, did you like my new toy?"
"It hurts. A lot."
"I know."
"I'm glad I tried it, but I'm not sure I like it that much. Do you mind?"
"Not at all. Shall we just keep it for special occasions then? I think it will come in useful when you need to be taught a lesson."
"Remind me to try to avoid that."
He nuzzled his face in her hair as he murmured his next words.
"You know I cherish you. You're my submissive and very precious to me. But one day, I *will* use this again, and I *will* hurt you. You need to understand that if you'll be wearing my collar."
Thea nodded, and reached for him. Immediately he gathered her up and held her against his chest.
"Fuck me now, Sir. Please. I need that."

"Do you want to be on top? In view of your delicate derriere?" He patted the region in question.

Thea yelped. "Yes, please."

Tony rolled onto his back, pulling her with him so she lay on top, face down, her body draped across his chest. "Grab a condom from the drawer." He indicated with his thumb where she would find the contraceptives. "Then I want you to remove my jeans and boxers, roll on the condom, and straddle me. I expect you to make a fine job of this, Mrs Richmond. Your customary attention to detail will be appreciated."

Thea needed no second telling. She scurried off the bed to locate a condom, then leaned across him to undo the zip on his jeans. The button at the waist was already open. She drew his jeans down his legs, and thanked him when he lifted first one then the other to ease her task. She dropped the discarded clothing on the floor and paused to admire his solid cock.

A naked Tony was a rare and beautiful sight. She knew him intimately, knew his moods, his preferences, his tastes. He had been inside her in every which way conceivable. He had explored every inch of her body, he was familiar with every intimate detail, there was no part of her he had not penetrated, used, pleasured, yet she would not have to take off a second glove to count the number of times she'd actually seen him naked. She was in no hurry to conclude the experience.

She crawled back onto the bed and knelt at his side. He looked at her, one eyebrow raised.

"Is there a problem, Thea? Some reason why you're not lowering your hot, wet cunt onto my cock right at this moment?"

She shook her head, and moved to straddle him. His hands at her waist stopped her.

"Thea? Tell me."

"How do you do that? Always know?"

"Like you said earlier, I'm a Dom who takes notice. So?"

"I just, it's just that I hardly ever get to see you—like this. You're beautiful."

"Kind words, Thea. And while we're exchanging pleasantries, so are you. Now we've established that, the reason you're not getting busy with that condom and jumping my bones is…?"

"I want to look."

"You are looking."

"I want to look some more. And touch you. I'd like to explore, and take my time. Like you do."

"I'm a Dom. You're a submissive so you do as you're told."

Disappointed, and chastened, Thea dropped her gaze. "Of course. I'm sorry, Sir." She tore the end off the foil wrapper she still clutched in her hand and reached for his thick, long cock.

"Okay. Take your time, as much as you want."

"Really?"

"Really. I haven't thanked you properly yet for the all-nighter you pulled yesterday. The least I can do is let you do this your way. I'm all yours."

"You mean that? You won't hurry me or suddenly grab me and…"

"Do *not* push your luck, Mrs Richmond. I promise to try. That's all." He lay back against the pillows and winked at her. Then he closed his eyes and folded his arms behind his head, the very picture of a relaxed male about to be pleasured.

Thea started as he so often did, at the top. She leaned across him to nibble her way from one shoulder to the other, allowing her breasts to scrape across his chest. He shifted under her, but remained in position. So far so good.

She shuffled a little bit further down, and flicked his left nipple with the tip of her tongue. It was flat, a dark pink button, hard but not obviously swollen and throbbing like her own. Even so, the contact did make him writhe a little. She tried again, this time on the other side. A low growl suggested to her that she may have even less time than she'd hoped. For a Dom whose patience seemed endless when drawing out her responses, he had a very low threshold when on the receiving end of a dose of erotic teasing himself.

Interesting.

Thea reached for his cock and wrapped her hand around it. At the base where it was thickest her fingers only just met. She squeezed and drew her hand up, stroking the entire length from base to tip.

Droplets appeared, and she smeared those across the smooth, round head. His erection jerked in her hand so she tightened her grip. She rubbed the pad of her thumb over the dark pink tip, loving the way he leaked more moisture onto her hand. She pumped her fist up and down the shaft several times, and watched his face contort as she did so. A submissive to her core, Thea nevertheless enjoyed the heady sense of power that his response gave her, the knowledge that she could do this to him. She held his pleasure in her hands, quite literally.

But she had more than her hands at her disposal. Holding his cock still, she wriggled lower and lay between his thighs, her face poised above him. She lowered her head and took his cock between her lips. At first she just sucked on the head, loving the salty taste of his pre-cum as he thrust upwards. Despite his declared good intentions he would soon retake control, she knew that.

Thea reached between his legs to cup his balls in her free hand, testing their weight, exploring the rougher texture of the skin of his scrotum. She closed her fingers around his nuts, squeezing their solid, rounded shape.

"Holy fuck, Thea. If you want me to fuck you, you need to move on. Now."

"Maybe I'm happy doing this."

"Thea…" His tone was low, gravelly, and dripped with lust-fuelled intent.

Thea was unmoved. He would do what he would do. She took even more of his cock into her mouth and sucked on it. She tilted her head to one side and was able to ease the head of his cock into the space inside her cheek, making room for yet more of the shaft. She had had less practice with oral sex than she would have liked, but she was propelled by instinct now, and encouraged by his groans and pants. He was becoming more vocal by the second. His hips were rocking, thrusting upwards in short, sharp stabs. Thea matched her own movements to his, synchronising their erotic dance as her hands and mouth worked on him.

His hand on her shoulder stopped her motion, but she continued to suck and to curl her tongue around the ridge just below the head. Her teeth scraped along the widest part of his cock, and she lapped the salty drops away. He was close, she knew that. But would he make her stop before…?

"Oh fuck. Fuck, fuck, *fuck*!" He thrust hard, his hand now on the back of her head to force greater penetration. No longer in control, Thea gripped for a moment, then opened her throat to allow him in. Heat hit the back of her mouth, her airway was blocked. She swallowed, once, then again, and dragged in several breaths through her nose. Tony held her still, fucking her mouth now. His balls tightened in her hand, his semen pumped out and splashed against her tonsils. She held on, sucked, swallowed, squeezed as he emptied himself into her willing mouth.

He went still, quiet. He fisted his hand in her hair and drew her head back. His cock sprang free.

"Are you okay? Was I too rough?"

"No, Sir. I'm glad you allowed me to finish."

"Sweetheart, you are *not* finished. Nowhere near. Did you lose that condom?"

"What, no. It's somewhere about…" She glanced to either side, spotting the foil poking out from a crease in the duvet. "Here it is, But are you still able to…"

"Give me a minute."

It was less than that. His erection hardly seemed to soften at all before she was unrolling the condom over his swelling, hardening shaft and positioning his solid length between her thighs. Thea straddled him, then lowered her body slowly. She used her fingers to direct the head of his cock into her entrance, then placed both hands on his shoulders as she sank onto him.

"Christ girl, you do a shit-hot blow job, but that feels so good. Squeeze me. Hard."

Thea obeyed, rotating her hips for good measure. Tony grabbed her waist to hold her still for a moment, then he thrust up. His cock filled her, stretching her, re-igniting the banked sensitivity he had so thoroughly cultivated earlier. She convulsed, and knew she would come in seconds. If he would allow it.

"Sir, may I…?"

"You may. As often as you want. Stroke your clit if it helps."

It would. It did. Thea rubbed the plump nubbin and dissolved into a delicious, languorous orgasm as Tony continued to stroke his cock in and out. He was in no hurry, their earlier frenzy now spent. Perhaps pumping his load into her mouth had taken the edge off for him. If so, she would reap the benefits now as he fucked her with slow, deliberate precision. He quickly found the perfect angle to drag his cock across her G-spot with every stroke. At this angle he could pull her down onto his cock to meet his upward thrusts, and with each driving plunge the head of his cock bumped her cervix. He was deep, as deep as she could recall, ever.

She squeezed her inner muscles again, caressing his cock with her body. He was big, stretching her, but it was perfect.

Her pussy spasmed, the prelude to another rocking climax. She leaned forward to rest her chin on his chest, unable to summon the energy to do her part any more and hoping he would take over.

He did. Tony flipped her onto her back without ever breaking contact. He hooked his arms under her legs, behind her knees and lifted her for his deeper penetration. He could have fucked her hard, on most occasions he would have. But not this time. He drew back, then slid his cock deep, the action gentle, exquisite in its tenderness.

"I love you." Thea whispered the words as her orgasm caught her again, but this time her release was achingly slow. Soft and gentle, the pleasure teased and soothed as her body offered up its response.

"I love you too, sub of mine." Tony buried his face in her neck and kissed her. His body stiffened. He buried his cock one last time, and held still. Wet heat filled the condom, and Thea held on. She promised herself she would never let him go.

Chapter eight

"So, what happened today? Did you report everything to the police yet?" Thea helped herself to another portion of sweet and sour pork as she glanced at Tony across the kitchen table.

"Certainly did. You have an Inspector Collywood very eager to talk to you. He's coming back tomorrow morning, around ten."

Thea nodded, her mouth full of aromatic noodles.

"And I have a somewhat twitchy finance department who'll need calming down. By the way, I read through Denise Metcalfe's personnel file after we talked earlier. I think you made a good call there. How come she was never promoted before?"

Thea swallowed her noodles and surveyed the array of foil trays spread across the table. She had her eye on a spring roll next.

"David Lister probably. If he was on the take, chances are other aspects of his management were suspect as well. Including his staff appraisals. Anyway, she'll have her chance to shine now, at least for a while."

"If she's any good she can keep the job. Call this a trial period."

Thea nodded again, this time impeded by a mouthful of crispy pastry and spicy vegetables. She chewed slowly, aware she was about to make another giant leap—for her.

"Shall I follow you to the office in the morning? In my car, I mean?"

Tony lifted an eyebrow, the only indication he gave that the significance of this moment was not lost on him. She was no longer insisting on working via remote access or only going into Dart Logistics' premises when the rest of the staff weren't there. He speared a piece of battered spicy chicken. "Why not travel in together? You *are* staying the night I assume?"

Thea put down her fork. "Yes, I'd like to. But I wouldn't want anyone getting the wrong idea. About us."

"Wrong idea?"

"Well, right idea then. But you know what I mean."

Tony grinned at her. "Yes, Mrs Richmond. I get your drift. That'll be fine. I was intending to go in early in any case, so you can take your time."

Thea picked up her utensil again, relieved he wasn't going to push her harder on this. He seemed ready to accept her baby steps. "I'll need to go home first, find some clothes suitable for work. I can hardly show up for my first day in jeans. Or worse still a corset and thong."

"Do you have a corset with you?" His eyes gleamed with interest.

"It's not your first day, technically. But I can see the corset would cause a stir in the warehouse. We'd probably have more than a few wrecked forklifts to worry about. Our insurance would go through the roof. No, you're quite right. We have enough difficulties to resolve just now without you adding to them by not adhering to the dress code."

Despite having started it Thea ignored the sensual banter, preferring to home in on the aspect of the conversation which mattered most to her at this moment. "As far as the rest of your staff are concerned, it's the first time they've seen me. First impressions and all that." Inwardly she grimaced, this was the part she dreaded most. Resolute, she suppressed her fears and concentrated on the conversation. "So, why are you going in early?"

"Morale's low. Yesterday everyone just feared the worst, and no one seemed that surprised at the prospect of Dart going under. They lack faith, and I intend to change that. I'll start by putting myself about, being seen out on the shop floor, so to speak. I want to get to know my staff and make sure they know me. I want to boost confidence, and develop a sense of pride, of ownership even amongst my teams. I want them to feel a part of Dart Logistics. Maybe then they won't steal from me."

"Most people aren't dishonest."

"No, I get that. But it won't hurt to win them over a little, get them on my side. Our side."

"Ah, a hearts and minds offensive then?"

"Yes, exactly. And while I'm doing that, you can be sorting out our backroom, make sure Dart Logistics has systems that work, policies that make sense, and we can enforce. And close any loopholes in our security. I want to be running a tight ship, and I intend for everyone who works for me to know that. Fair, but firm. I intend for

Dart to be a great place to work, but a lousy place if you're idle or feel like putting your hand in the till."

"More carrot and stick than hearts and minds, then?" Another spring roll found its way onto Thea's plate.

Tony shrugged as he poured them both a second glass of the complementary cola that came with their meal. "Maybe, though I do subscribe to the UN maxim on international peacekeeping—when you have them by the balls, their hearts and minds *will* follow."

Thea arched one expressive eyebrow. "I rather like getting up close and personal with your balls, Sir, but I'm not sure about the rest of that analogy."

Tony stood and leaned across the table to kiss her hair. "You need to become a little less fastidious, but I have every faith in you, Mrs Richmond. We'll make a great team."

*****

"Which office would you like me to use?" Thea stood in his doorway, her briefcase dangling from her right hand. She was dressed in a tight-fitting navy blue suit, the jacket buttoned over a crisp white shirt. Her hair was drawn back into a neat, if rather severe chignon, and her black leather court shoes gleamed. She looked formidable, formal, and sexy as hell when he considered the lush, curvy body which he knew for certain was to be found beneath those austere layers. His cock leapt to attention.

"Shit, you look—different."

Thea narrowed her eyes, and flicked them briefly to her left, indicating the presence of Isabel nearby. "My office?"

"You can share mine, at least for now. I don't intend to be in here that much." Tony stood and gestured to the chair he just vacated. "Did you speak to Mrs Metcalfe yet?"

"No. That's my first job. I should be able to get that out of the way before the police arrive."

Tony nodded as he passed her to lean around the doorway to the outer office. "Isabel, could you arrange for a second desk to be set up in here please? And I think Mrs Richmond will need you to locate

Denise Metcalfe and have her come up here. Have we heard anything more from Inspector Collywood?"

His PA glanced up from the post she was opening, her expression stony. "Yes, yes, and no."

Tony nodded, choosing to ignore her curt tone. "Right. And is there any chance of some coffee? Perhaps you'd like to join us."

His PA's expression warmed. "Right on it. How does Mrs Richmond take hers?"

Tony was relieved at the bright smile she shot him as she got to her feet and made a mental note to find ways of reassuring Isabel that her position was not about to be usurped.

Tony and Isabel both sat in on the interview with Inspector Collywood, but Tony had to admit it was entirely Thea's show. And she handled it like the absolute pro she was. Their relationship outside of work was a bonus, and a seriously hefty bonus at that, but here in the work environment she was just awesome. She knew her stuff, could deal with every issue raised, understood her evidence, and the implications of every fine detail. The officers appeared perfectly satisfied that there was a case to answer. They left, on their way to pick up the three suspects and question them.

"Do you think we'll have David Lister badgering us again? He's already phoned three times this morning, and I can't count how many emails he's sent." Isabel folded her notes into a tidy stack and rose to leave too.

Tony nodded. "Probably. Almost certainly once the police let him go. Just keep on fielding his calls if you would please. Neither me nor Thea intend to talk to him."

Thea glared at him. "Would you like me to start my audit of your human resources policies now, *Mr diMarco*?" She emphasised his name, particularly his title.

Tony managed to conceal his grin. So, his little sub wanted to keep things formal here, did she? He'd indulge her, up to a point. But she'd earned a spanking later. The first of several if he was any judge. He pulled a small block of post-it notes toward him and jotted a few words on the top one. He tore it from the block and stuck it on her leather-bound document folder.

Later. Dining table. Your bare bottom, my belt. xxx
Tony enjoyed a private moment of pure lust as her face coloured puce. He beamed a smile at a speechless Thea as he sauntered out of the room, nodded to Isabel in the outer office, and headed back down into the warehouse to charm his employees.

"I didn't get chance to ask you earlier, how did it go with Denise Metcalfe?" Tony leaned back in his chair and placed his feet on the desk. He surveyed his new colleague as she closed down the recently installed computer terminal on her pristine desk. Isabel, with her customary efficiency, had had the additional furniture and equipment delivered and set up within hours of him requesting it. Thea looked quite at home already.
"Great, once she calmed down. She was convinced I'd called her in because of the investigation, which of course was true indirectly. She looked astonished though when I offered her the job."
"She accepted?"
"Oh yes, but we'll need to find some management training for her. She's a good accountant, but as we already know, there's more to her new role than that."
"I'm sure you'll come up with something suitable."
"Me? So is staff training my responsibility too?" She swivelled her chair round to face him.
"Part of human resources, surely."
"I suppose." She picked up a pen and turned back to her desk to jot a note on a sheet of paper.
"Don't you use an electronic diary?"
"Yes, for some things. But I like lists. On paper. It's a system that works."
Tony shrugged. "Whatever. Who am I to quarrel? But I will require you to turn your desk around, I prefer you facing me."
She swivelled again and looked up, peering at him over her glasses. "What, you want me to do that now?"
"No, next time you're in. Which will be when?"

"It's Tuesday today. I need to go in to Kershaw's tomorrow, certainly, and probably Thursday too. I'll be here again on Friday though, all being well."

He nodded. "Bring a weekend bag with you. You'll be staying at mine. So, are you ready for the off?"

"Almost. I just need to rinse these cups and—"

"Leave them. We have a cleaner who does that stuff. Come here."

"Tony…?"

"Here. Now." His tone held that curt Dom timbre. She rose and crossed the room.

"Sir, I don't think—"

"You look very prim, Mrs Richmond. Tell me, are you wearing knickers under that oh-so-decent skirt?"

"Of course, Sir."

"Commendable. Remove them please. And the tights too, obviously."

"I will not. Not here."

"Oh Thea…" His tone was deliberately ominous, dripping sensual menace. "You know better than that."

"Sir, I don't mean to be difficult. Or disobedient. But…"

"We are quite alone here, Thea. I promised you a spanking, but I'll deliver that at home. And incidentally, the six strokes I had in mind just doubled. But I want your underwear now."

He held out his hand for her knickers, and watched with interest as a parade of emotions crossed her face. Alarm, confusion. And perhaps arousal. Yes, definitely arousal. She stepped out of those sexy, understated little shoes and bent to lift her skirt, then rolled down her tights from under it. She offered those to him, and he accepted them. His intention was that she be naked under her suit. He waited while she peeled her panties down her legs too, then pocketed both garments.

"Are you wet, Thea?"

"Yes, Sir." She stood before him, her expression despondent.

"Why so sad? Is this not a cause for celebration?"

"Not here. It's okay if we're somewhere we can fuck, but—"

"I don't usually fuck my colleagues, but I suppose I could accommodate you. If you insist."

"That's not what I meant, Sir."
"No? Are you not wet then? Disgracefully so? Not dripping in readiness for a long, sweet fuck?"
"Sir, I can't do this." She raised her gaze to his, the telltale sheen of tears unmistakable.
"Why? Tell me, Thea."
"What if someone were to see? What if Isabel had to come back for something?"
"The outer doors are locked. There's no CCTV in here. No one's going to see. No one's coming in. You're safe, Thea. Well, comparatively so. I suppose that does depend on how far you decide to defy me."
"I'm not defying you. I wouldn't. You know that. Please…"
He reached for her, cupped her chin in his hand. She went silent instantly, her expression calming at the contact.
"Let me worry, you just obey. Yes?"
Her nod was almost imperceptible, but enough. Her submission, given anyway, despite her fears.
"Lift your skirt, and bend over my desk then. Now please."
Thea made no further protest, just edged around him and did exactly as he'd instructed. Tony watched as her beautiful bottom adorned his workspace, lifted and ready for him. He would enjoy punishing her later. But for now, he stepped forward and parted her buttocks with his hands.
She sighed and settled more comfortably on the desk, her body relaxing, becoming limp almost. Her hands were outstretched, gripping the opposite edge. As he stroked his fingers down the groove between her cheeks he watched her fingers loosen as she sank more deeply into her submissive haze. He was surprised, it usually required some serious attention with a flogger or paddle to get her to this point. On this occasion the pain had been mental, emotional, but she was coming through it, digging within herself to find the trust she needed in order to respond to him. He was not about to disappoint her.
He undid his trousers to release his cock, and sheathed himself fast. He stepped closer, tapping her bare feet with his leather-shod one to encourage her to widen her stance. Then he reached between

her legs to stroke her pussy, from front to back. He took his time, allowing his fingertips to dip inside her entrance, and linger there. She was not exaggerating about her wetness. He smeared her juices across her arse, and considered fucking her there instead. No, her pussy was drooling. She needed this. Using both hands now he parted the lips of her pussy and positioned his cock at her entrance. She rocked her hips slightly, pushing back against him. He tapped her bottom, a mild rebuke to remind her who was in control here. She lifted her bottom slightly, a silent plea, and went still.

Tony dislodged the clips holding her hair in place and unravelled her neat chignon. He spread her hair across his desk, then he pressed the head of his cock into her, and waited. She squeezed, tensing her inner muscles, her body shuddering with unmet need. He shifted and pressed forward again. A little more, another inch, then another. She was panting now, her eyes closed. He eased back, almost leaving her, then forward again. He repeated, a series of short, stabbing strokes, teasing, promising, tormenting. Her breath hitched, caught in her throat. She was desperate, needy, utterly his. He plunged, sinking his solid erection right to the hilt. She let out a sharp cry, somewhere between shock and relief. He pulled back and drove into her again to set up a pounding rhythm. Her pussy tightened around him, he knew she was on the verge of coming. He hadn't given permission, and he wondered if she would seek his consent. He'd say no, because she needed to be controlled right now. She craved his dominance and needed to please him, win his approval. For that he had to set her a challenge.

"Sir, I needed to orgasm."

"No, Thea. Not yet."

"Sir, yes! Now. I can't help it."

"No. Wait."

Her body was rigid, straining as her inner battle was played out. She was gripping the edge of the desk, her breath coming in short, staccato gasps. He slowed his thrusts, again opting for the short, rapid strokes which drove her into a frenzy of clenching. Her hips thrust back against him, but he didn't admonish her this time. She was trying to obey him, struggling to hold on to control of her response. He intended to test that control to the limit. Leaning over her slightly he reached around and under to lay his middle finger across her swollen clit.

She shook her head, her expression pleading now as she opened her eyes to look up at him over her shoulder. "Please Sir, don't. Don't do that."

"I'll do what I want to you, Thea. You know that. You love it when I stroke your clit."

"Sir, I can't take any more. Please let me come."

"Soon. But first..."

He circled her clit with his finger, the caress slow, light, barely there. Thea whimpered, her cunt contracting hard around his cock. He drove forward, filling her completely, then stroked the tip of her clit again. He applied just a touch more pressure, and she started to convulse. He stopped, waited. She hauled herself back from the brink, her entire body shivering. Tony waited for a count of five, then another. He leaned in to murmur in her ear.

"Come now, Thea."

His finger hovered, a fraction of a millimetre from her clit. His cock stretched and shaped her. He kissed the back of her neck, then dragged his teeth across her sensitive skin. It was enough, too much. She convulsed around him as her orgasm seized and spun her. Tony rubbed her clit at last to provide the friction she craved, driving her release further, harder, deeper.

At last she lay still under him, spent. He took a handful of her hair and twisted it around his fist, lifting her face from the table top. He leaned over and kissed her on the mouth, hard. He plunged his tongue between her lips, tasting, exploring, possessing her even now. He broke the kiss and started to move again, driving his cock deep with the long, slow strokes he loved. His own climax was just seconds away, but he'd been determined to see hers through first. Her pussy was tight, so hot, so wet. She seemed to squeeze around him, was she doing it on purpose? Yes, probably. He tightened his grip on her hair and growled into her ear.

"Behave."

She relaxed, giving over control to him totally. Her submission was all he required to cause his nuts to contract. Semen surged into the condom and his balls emptied.

Still holding her by the hair he nudged her nose with his. "Talk to me, little sub. Are you okay?"

"Yes Sir. Thank you for that."

"For what, exactly?"

"For forcing the issue, for making me do this. Here."

"Was it worth it? Worth affronting Mrs Richmond's delicate sensitivities?"

"Not so much delicate, more…" She hesitated, seemed to be searching for the word. Tony could have supplied something but opted to wait, to see what she came up with. Her choice pleased him. "… rigid."

"I'd say you were far from rigid now, Mrs Richmond. Yielding would be a better description."

"I like yielding."

"I know. So we'll be doing it again then?"

"If you like, Sir. Your choice."

He straightened and released her hair, then withdrew from her. He took a moment to deal with the condom and rearrange his clothing, then helped her to stand upright too. Her skirt fell back into place, the look almost decent. If her just-fucked hair wasn't such a giveaway. And her bare legs. He wanted to get her home. Fast.

"Exactly. So, my place then? I still owe you a decent spanking."

"Thank you, Sir. That will be nice."

Chapter nine

"You need to reinstate Jeremy Malone."
"Who?" Tony regarded Thea across the conference table, as four more pairs of puzzled eyes also stared at her.
"Jeremy Malone. The man you paid compensation to. For wrongful dismissal." Unruffled, Thea supplied the clarification.
"No way!" This from Isabel. As Tony's PA she usually attended senior staff meetings and took any notes. She also contributed to the discussion when she had a point to make. Now seemed to be one such occasion. Thea inclined her head to acknowledge the comment.
The others present were Denise Metcalfe, just settling into her new job as Head of Finance, now with three weeks of experience in the role under her belt. Thea was delighted with Denise's performance so far and privately blessed the day she suggested her promotion to Tony. Next to Denise sat Eric Henderson, these days only heading up their corporate IT since Thea had relieved him of the human resources role. He'd been delighted to the rid of it, and had fallen over himself to support the new incumbent, another internal promotion. Christopher McCoy had been in his new post for a total of three and a half days and was still somewhat shell-shocked by his rapid rise from the ranks of HR admin. Even so, Thea believed he'd do very well. Christopher shared her passion for the detail, but he had a feel for the human stories too. She hoped for his support in this coming debate over their ex-employee.
Isabel wasn't done. "Why? Why would we want to do that? The man was a waster. A liability. And he's gone. History."
Thea did not miss the looks exchanged between Denise and Christopher at Isabel's remark. It seemed they at least did not buy in to this notion. Tony's expression on the other hand suggested he was inclined to agree with his faithful secretary's analysis, but he still regarded Thea with some interest. "What's this about, Mrs Richmond?"
She met his gaze levelly. "I never met Mr Malone. Did you?"
Tony shook his head. "No. He'd been dismissed before I bought Dart. I just got caught in the fallout afterwards."

"What about the rest of you? Did any of you know him? Talk to him?" Thea addressed this question to the others around the table, but her gaze rested on Denise and Christopher. Nevertheless, it was Eric who responded first.

The man nodded. "Yes, I dealt with his appeal following his disciplinary hearing. I interviewed him, and could hardly get a word out of him, to be fair. I didn't get the impression he particularly wanted to save his job."

Isabel chipped in again. "Exactly. He saw a chance to screw some cash out of the company instead, without the bother of working for it."

Thea ignored Isabel's comment this time and directed her attention to the two remaining managers who had not yet spoken. "Chris, Denise, did either of you know Mr Malone personally?"

Both nodded. Christopher opted to speak first. "He was a quiet enough bloke, kept himself to himself, but he was fairly popular as far as I knew. I was surprised, actually, that he'd got himself into so much bother. It didn't seem his style, somehow."

Denise nodded. "That was my impression too. There was a bit of gossip at the time, you know the sort of thing. Water cooler chat."

This attracted Tony's attention. "What chat? What were people saying?"

Denise warmed to her theme. "Well, that he'd had a raw deal, really. He was a loner, but he worked hard and people liked him." She turned to face Isabel, and her tone hardened. "And he wasn't a waster. Definitely not. His team ran like clockwork, and he was always working late. That's what seemed most odd, that he was in trouble for poor time-keeping, when he actually worked all the hours God sent."

Tony was frowning, looking from Chris to Denise, then to Eric. "Was this discussed at the hearing, or in his appeal?"

Eric shook his head. "First I've heard of any of it. I wasn't at the first hearing in any case. But I read the file notes and none of this was in there. He never tried to present any mitigating factors at the appeal. He hardly said a word at all."

Tony turned to Thea, his expression intent. "Mrs Richmond, am I to gather you've been listening to water cooler chat?"

"I have, yes. It's what you pay me for, to get under the skin of how this place runs and fix it. I got wind of the disquiet that still exists out there about Jeremy Malone's sacking, so I did a bit of digging around, background information, that sort of thing."

Tony leaned back, his posture relaxed, his expression anything but. "And you came up with...?"

Thea opened her notebook and poised her pen. "First, can I check out a couple more details? Eric, who represented Mr Malone during the disciplinary process?"

Eric shrugged. "No one. He was entitled to have a union rep or a colleague present but he didn't take that up."

Thea perched her glasses on her nose and scribbled few lines, then turned to Eric again. "Did he know he was allowed to have someone with him?"

"I expect so. Everyone knows that sort of stuff."

"No they don't." Chris leaned forward, his gaze intent. "You'd be astonished how little people tend to know about their rights. Especially when they're under pressure."

Thea smiled at her latest recruit. The lad would go far.

Eric frowned, but his demeanour seemed somewhat defensive to Thea. She regretted that, her purpose was not to re-open the previous shortcomings of their HR department, but she sensed an ongoing problem and was determined to address it. Eric leaned forward, his words directed at Tony. "We wrote to him. Everything was done by the book."

Tony shook his head slowly. "Eric, it wasn't. You know that, we all know it. That's why the tribunal stung me for twenty five grand."

Isabel tossed her pencil onto the meeting table. It fell with a clatter. "It's done with. Over. It was a costly mistake, but one we won't repeat. We should leave it and move on." The exasperation was apparent in Isabel's tone, in her frustrated tapping of the table top with her manicured fingernails.

"It isn't though. Over." Thea's quiet tone held everyone's attention, especially Tony's. "It won't be over as long as we have staff, a lot of staff in fact, who believe we did that man an injustice. The compensation doesn't change anything, not as far as they're concerned. Resentment festers. We need loyalty, and commitment from the people we employ. They expect the same from us."

Isabel opened her mouth to issue another protest but Tony forestalled that with a lifted hand. "Thea, go on please. What more do you have to tell us about this matter?"

"Jeremy Malone wasn't married, was he?"

"No. His wife died about three years ago. Cancer I think." Denise supplied this information. "We all had a whip round."

"Does he have other family?"

Denise shook her head. "Not to my knowledge." She looked to Eric and Chris for further elaboration. The doubtful expressions suggested none would be forthcoming.

Thea consulted her notebook again. "In fact, Mr Malone has a daughter. Melanie, aged twelve. She has Downs syndrome."

Tony abandoned his relaxed pose. Elbows on the table he fixed Thea with a familiar, focused stare. "A lone parent, of a child with special needs? And you're telling me we didn't know that?"

"Well, I certainly didn't know." Eric was quick to chip in.

"Would it have made a difference? If you had known?" Thea's question might have been addressed to Eric, but it was Tony who she was watching, whose reaction mattered now.

"I reckon it would. The company would have cut him more slack probably." This from Tony. "Is there more, Thea?"

Sensing she was on the downhill slope now, Thea continued. "Yes. As you say, Chris, Mr Malone was a bit of a loner. However it seems he was close to a Mr Bartlett. Albert Bartlett, who retired three years ago."

Chris nodded. "He might have been. I was new then but I do remember old Albert. He was Jeremy's boss, and Jeremy took over his team when Albert went off to look after his roses or whatever."

"That's right." Thea was no longer referring to her notes. She gazed around the table at the people listening to her. "I found Albert's contact details in our records and rang him up. I asked him if he could shed any light on what might have gone wrong. He was very helpful. It seems Melanie attends a residential facility during the week and comes home each weekend. She arrives on Friday afternoon and leaves again on Monday morning. Jeremy always had to be home by three o'clock on Friday because that was when Melanie's taxi would drop her off, and she wouldn't be picked up again until nine thirty on Monday. So he left work early on Friday's and was late every Monday."

"Shit! Fucking shit. How come none of this came out?" Tony's voice was a low growl. Thea had heard that tone before, but this time it was not directed at her. Even so, her pussy clenched.

Eric was the one to answer. "Search me, boss. I'd have upheld his appeal for sure if I'd had any inkling. Bloody hell!" To his credit, the man looked devastated.

"Do we know for sure this is the reason for the pattern of absenteeism?" Denise was making feverish notes of her own now. Thea smiled at her. The question was exactly the right one to raise at this stage. "Not without talking to him. But I think that should be our next step. I'm happy to do it."

Denise flattened her lips thoughtfully. "You don't have to. I will if you like. Or I could come with you."

A resounding crack disturbed their conversation. Isabel had snapped her pencil. All eyes turned to the agitated PA.

"What the hell would be the point? He was badly treated, probably. Okay, I get that. But he had his compensation. He was paid out. It's not as though there's anything else we could do about it now. I say we drop it, learn from it, and move on."

Thea stiffened and turned to address the woman directly. In her view it was time Isabel Barnard wound her neck in over this. The woman hadn't a clue what she was talking about.

"There are several things we could do. One, we can review how we managed to miss such a vital piece of relevant information. We need to understand how it was that we had someone working for us, whose personal circumstances were so difficult, and impacted on his job, and we knew nothing about it. No allowances made, nothing. Two, we could even now review the disciplinary action taken and revise our findings if we think there's a case for that. And three, we could offer Mr Malone his job back."

"His job back? That's ridiculous. What about the money he got from us. Is he going to give that back?"

Thea opened her mouth, but again Tony halted the conversation by simply lifting his hand. "There will be no giving back the money. That was his compensation, awarded lawfully. But we do owe it to the people who still work for us, and to Mr Malone, to get to the bottom of what actually went on. I've heard enough to convince me we should look again at this matter, and I'd like you all to leave this with me for now. I'll consider what further action needs to be taken. If any."

When both Thea and Isabel would have offered further argument he stood. "Thank you, everyone. And thank you especially, Mrs Richmond for bringing this matter back to our attention. I think we all have work to do now, do we not?"

They were dismissed, including her. Thea stood and would have filed out of the meeting room with the rest but Tony called her back.

"One moment, Mrs Richmond. If you please. And would you mind closing the door?"

Thea did as he asked, and returned to stand before the table. Tony remained seated, at its head.

"Mrs Richmond, I make this three nights you haven't stayed at my house. Why is that?"

"I've been working at Kershaw's, you know that. And not finishing until after eight most evenings. Holding down two jobs is hard work."

"I get that. Maybe you need to relax more."

"Perhaps. Do you have something in mind, Sir?" The shift was subtle, but irresistible. When he looked at her like that, when his tone took on that unrelenting Dom timbre, when his body language exuded power and control, she melted into her submissive mindset. It no longer mattered that they were in the office. He was her Dom, her Master, and she responded in the only way she could.

"I do. I'd like you to meet me at The Wicked Club this evening. Say around nine."

"Very well, Sir."

"And you'll be sleeping with me tonight, at my house, so make sure you bring clothes for tomorrow and anything else you might need."

"Of course, Sir. Thank you."

"You're welcome. I should say, you look very nice today, Thea. Is that a new dress?"

"Yes, Sir."

"It's very—smart. Formal. Very suitable for the office. Tell me, Thea, what do you wear under such a respectable outfit?"

"An uplift bra, and a thong, Sir. And stockings of course."

"Of course. Show me please."

"You want me to take off my dress Sir? Here?"

"How else will you show me your delightfully sexy underwear, Mrs Richmond? It is delightfully sexy I assume?"

"I believe so, Sir."

He offered no further comment, just raised one eyebrow and waited. He did not appear patient.

Thea fumbled with the zipper at the back of her dress, but in seconds had managed to unfasten it and slid the burgundy fabric from her shoulders. The bodice of her dress dropped to her waist, then with the help of a slight shove the entire garment pooled on the floor. She stepped from the heap of dark red to stand closer to Tony.

He scrutinised her pale pink lacy bra, cut to reveal the upper curves of her breasts and only just covering her swollen nipples, then ran his gaze lower to take in the matching thong and barely black lace topped stockings. He twirled his finger, and she turned around to show him her rear.

"No bruises I see."

"There were. They were lovely, but they faded."

"I see. I'll refresh those for you tonight."

"Thank you, Sir. I'll look forward to that."

"I know you will, Mrs Richmond. Now, before you go, would you lean forward please? You can rest your hands on the table if you need to."

Thea did as he asked.

Tony got to his feet at last and stood behind her. "Spread your legs, sub."

She obeyed, widening her stance as far as she could, beyond what felt comfortable. She chewed on her lower lip as Tony slid his hand between her legs to tug her thong to one side. He plunged two, then three fingers inside her, scissoring them against her quivering inner walls. She stifled a gasp as her already wet cunt drooled in response.

As quickly as he had shoved his fingers into her, Tony withdrew them. "Stand up and turn round,"

Thea did so.

"Open your mouth."

Again, she obeyed.

He licked the fingers he had just fucked her with, and smiled. "You taste so good, little sub. My perfect whore. Now you try."

He put his fingers in her mouth. Thea tasted her own juices, musky, rich and slightly spicy. She closed her lips around his digits and sucked, curling her tongue around them to lap off every last trace of her cream. He allowed her to finish before he pulled his hand from her mouth. He smiled at her, a smile of pleasure, of acceptance. Thea warmed within the comforting haze of his approval, and fought the urge to reach up and kiss his lips.

Tony simply offered her the slightest nod, then stepped back. "You may put your dress back on, Thea."

Her hands trembled as she did so, so much that Tony had to assist her in zipping it up. At last, perfectly respectable once more, she faced him. "Should I go back to work now, Sir?"

"Yes. And Mrs Richmond, thank you. For earlier, about Jeremy Malone. I appreciate that."

Thea made no further comment. She just smiled, bowed her head, and floated from the room.

Chapter ten

"Sir? Am I late?" Thea approached Tony across the entrance foyer of The Wicked Club, and sank to her knees in front of him. He was pleased to note that she had already deposited her overcoat and bag in the cloakroom so was wearing just a vivid red corset which laced up the front, a thong, matching crimson stockings and spiky stiletto heels.

"No Thea. You're exactly on time. I expected no less." He caressed her head, running his fingers through the silky curls of her unbound hair. He loved her hair, especially when it was loose like this though he might need to tie it up later. Such a contrast to her prim and proper, and oh-so-restrained office persona, though these days she seemed much more relaxed whichever setting she was in. He liked to think he'd had something to do with that, with helping her to be comfortable in her skin.

"Thank you." She lifted her gaze to meet his eyes, her expression warm and so sexy. He knew without needing to ask that her body was responding already, her pussy moistening for him.

"Would you like a drink, or shall we go straight to the dungeon?" Tony placed two fingers under her chin to hold her face still, not that she showed any inclination to move.

"A glass of water would be very welcome, Sir."

Good answer. He set great store by hydration. And anticipation. He also had a personal matter of some importance to raise with her.

"The bar first, then. Come." He turned and walked away from her. He had no need to look behind him to know that Thea had risen to her feet and followed him.

They sat beside each other in low chairs in a corner of the club's alcohol-free bar. Thea sipped her water, Tony had fruit juice.

He regarded her thoughtfully. "What would you like from me tonight, Thea?"

"Your choice, Sir, as always." She dropped her gaze, a gesture of respect, of her submission to his control. His cock leapt to attention. *Christ, she was lovely.*

He loved her submission, but what he wanted to discuss required eye contact so he tipped her chin up with his fingers. "I'm thinking something quite intense. I want to hear you squeal. And I intend to leave you with plenty of new bruises to reflect on later. A souvenir of a pleasant evening."

Thea smiled and held his gaze. "I expected no less, Sir. Thank you."

"And whilst we're discussing souvenirs, I have something for you." He reached into the pocket of his sharp, grey suit trousers and withdrew a long, narrow box. A jewellery case. He held it out to her.

Thea took the box and held it in both her hands. "There's no need to buy me presents, Sir."

"This isn't a present, little sub. At least not in the sense you mean. Open it."

Thea flicked back the lid, and gasped. She looked up at him, wide-eyed. "Is this what I think it is?"

He nodded. "A collar. But this one's suitable to wear all the time. Which is what I expect of you. We discussed this before, but now I need to be sure you fully understand. If you agree, once I fasten it around your neck, only I can remove it."

"It's lovely Sir. Absolutely beautiful."

Tony was pleased. He'd thought the elegant leather and gold design he'd had custom made for her would appeal to Thea. The locking mechanism, though secure, was discreet and the piece was an attractive item of jewellery. They would both recognise its significance, as would others in their lifestyle. But there was nothing about it to compromise the privacy he knew to be so precious to Thea.

"So, you will wear it then? No change of heart?"

"Of course I'll wear it, Sir. I'd be honoured."

"That makes two of us. Are you ready then?"

Thea nodded.

"Lift up your hair please, and turn around."

He took the box back from her, and Thea did as he asked. Despite her composure when she first entered the club and knelt before him he noticed that her hands were shaking now. He extracted the collar from the satin lining and dangled it between his fingers.

"Are you certain, Thea? This is a big decision. From here, there's no going back. Not for either of us."

"I don't want to go back."

"By allowing me to lock this around your neck, you're accepting that I will control you from now on. This is a permanent symbol of your submission to me. It makes me your Master."

"You are already that, Sir. My Master. The collar just acknowledges the way I feel. The way I've always felt about you."

"And by giving this to you I'm making a statement too, about the way I feel. You know I love you, don't you? That I'll protect you, always. I'll never harm you. I'll do all in my power to give you what you need, even when you don't know yourself what that is."

"I do know that Master. I trust you. I love you."

Tony kissed the exposed nape of her neck, then slipped the collar around the slender column. He snapped the locking rings into place and released the strip of corded leather and gold to drape around her throat. The collar was light, and long enough to be comfortable. Thea lifted her hands to finger the narrow length.

"How does it feel?"

"It feels wonderful, Sir. I love it."

"Some couples prefer a formal collaring ceremony. We could do that, if you like."

She shook her head. "I don't feel the need for that, unless you want to. I know how this is, between us. I don't need anyone else to formalise it."

He was pleased to hear that, not being especially given to public declarations himself. Still, he wanted to explore this with her, be sure they were in agreement. "What about marriage? The usual, vanilla way."

She turned to him, her expression surprised, before she seemed to remember her submissive manners and dropped her gaze. "I had never considered that, Sir."

He took her hand and squeezed. Thea bowed her head lower to rest her cheek on his wrist.

He leaned forward too, modulating his voice to a murmur, for her ears alone. "This arrangement we now have is as binding as any marriage. You know that and I know it. But it's private. Others won't be aware this bond exists between us, even within the D/s community. That could be awkward—at work for example. Or if we have children.

She turned her head to look at him. "Children? Do you want kids?"
"We've never talked about it. But in the future, we might. Who knows what might happen?"
"I don't mind being married. If you think we should."
He grinned at her. "Such enthusiasm for the married state. Your traditional approach is refreshing. Shall we just agree it's a possibility, if it seems expedient? Later."
Thea nodded. "Yes, Sir. Later."
"So, now I believe we have something to celebrate. The dungeon I think."

*****

"Hold out your hands, Thea."
She did so, and Tony fastened a leather cuff around each of her wrists. He knew she particularly liked this pair, they had a soft lining, very comfortable. He intended her to become a lot less comfortable in the next few minutes, but he was happy to start by playing nice.
"Hands above your head please."
Again she obeyed without question. He attached the clips on each of her cuffs to a large metal ring suspended from the ceiling in the dungeon. He adjusted the height of it so that she was pulled up onto her toes, even higher than the lift provided by her sexy heels. She was stretched out before him, her body on display, in full view of any other members who wanted to watch their play. In recent weeks he'd come to appreciate the special intimacy of their private scenes, but he still loved the freedom of scening in public, the decadent, rule-breaking, taboo-busting escapism of it. He knew this was much of the buzz for Thea too. That and sub-space, obviously.
"I'm going to blindfold you." It was a statement, not a request. He bent to retrieve a black silk scarf from his bag, in preference to a leather blindfold., Again, he knew which Thea liked best and he was inclined to indulge her. For now. He stepped up behind her and secured the scarf over her eyes.
"Now the corset. It's breathtaking, but it has to go."
"What about the rules?"

No nudity was allowed in the public areas of the club, but pretty much anything short of that was accepted. "I'll leave your thong. And your shoes. And this of course." He flicked her new collar with the tips of his fingers, admiring the glint of the gold as it was reflected in the subdued floor mounted lighting.

Thea simply nodded. He couldn't discern her expression really, due to the blindfold, and her body was effectively immobile now. But there was a relaxed, easy looseness about her that betrayed her mood. She was slipping into her submissive mindset, already drifting in a contented haze. She'd always been responsive, always easy to please. Perhaps too easy. Her mental block over using safe words bothered him. It called for extra vigilance on his part but so far he hadn't slipped up. And he wouldn't. He adored Thea, it was that simple. He would never let her down.

He loosened the laces which held the corset secure, unthreading them from the eyelets to remove it from her body. Her naked breasts quivered, just below his eye level in her current elevated position. Her nipples were pink, and already swollen. He had plans for those tender buds. Soon. Very soon.

He circled her, taking his time as he admired the athletic lines of her body. As far as he was aware Thea didn't work out, but she was still toned and slender, though with curves just where he liked to find them. Her bum especially, so round and peachy, the soft skin a blank canvas for him to etch his marks upon. He caressed her buttocks with his palm, first one, then the other. Then he delivered a sharp slap to her left cheek, which he quickly rubbed away.

Thea trembled, her anticipation building.

Tony slapped her other buttock, and rubbed again. He could have sworn she moaned. Time to ramp things up.

He delved into his bag again, this time producing a flogger. Not the gentle suede one he'd teased her with before. This one was heavier, the fronds made of soft leather. It would deliver a sharper caress, a little more bite, just to get her attention.

He started on her shoulders, at first stroking, then introducing a sharp flick of his wrist to send the leather strands snaking across her skin. She hissed, he knew it hurt. Not a lot, but enough. He spent a few minutes warming her up, then moved around to the front. The flogger left faint pink lines across her breasts, criss-crossing, a delicate pattern emerging under his careful ministrations. He loved the way her flesh rippled as he struck her, her nipples hardening as the flogger curled around them.

He moved down to her stomach, then her hips. He circled again, dropping delicate strokes across her bottom and thighs.

Thea was writhing from side to side, following rather than evading his blows. At the first sign of hesitancy on her part he would have stopped, but there was none. She was loving this. So far so good, but now it was time to raise the stakes farther.

He bent to peer into his bag again, and found the toys for the next stage of the scene he had planned—a pair of nipple clamps, and a tawse. He pocketed the clamps and tossed the tawse onto the floor in front of Thea, then he returned to stand before his helpless, panting submissive. Would he tell her what he was going to do next? No, he thought not. The blindfold was signal enough that she wasn't to know what he was doing to her. She was to just feel. And respond. Words between them would break the mood. She was in her own zone, he was in control, she trusted him. No words were needed.

He cupped her right breast in his hand, feeling the weight, lifting it. He bent his head to take her nipple in his mouth and sucked on it. She arched her back, thrusting her breasts at him. He wrapped his tongue around the hard bud, then grazed it with his teeth. She flinched, he paused. She arched her back again, subconsciously urging him to continue. He took the pebbling nub between his teeth and bit, hard enough to hurt. She let out a squeal, the first of many he would hear from her in the coming hour or so he hoped.

He released her and stepped back to admire his handiwork so far. He wasn't satisfied. He wanted it harder, more swollen. More pain. He took her nipple between his finger and thumb, and twisted. Thea screamed.

"Sir, sir!"

"Too much?"

She shook her head, but he knew. As always, he knew. He pulled the nipple clamps from his pocket and allowed the chain linking them to drape between his fingers. He slipped the ring over her nipple and turned the tightening screw slowly, watching her face as he did so. Her mouth was the only part visible, but he caught the pursing of her lips, then the grimace as the pain really started to bite. She whimpered, and he stopped.

He left the clamped nipple to attend to the other, repeating his actions until he was satisfied it was sufficiently pebbled. He intended her to fully appreciate the impact of the toys he'd brought for her. He slipped the second clamp into place and tightened it as he had the first.

He stood back again, and raked her body with his eyes. It never failed to impress him, the sight of a lovely woman bound for his pleasure, her nipples clamped, occasionally her clit too, though that was not his intention today. Too personal, too intimate for here. He would save that for later. At home. When he could fuck her arse to his—and her—heart's content. The management at the club took a dim view of couples actually screwing in the dungeon, though more or less everything else would be tolerated.

He moved in close again and palmed her breasts, squeezing the lower curves. He pressed them together to create a deep cleavage, and buried his nose in that. Thea groaned, her discomfort increasing by the second, every movement of her tortured nipples excruciating for her.

"Do you want to stop yet, sub? Had enough?" He knew the answer, could tell by her slack mouth, by the way she ran her tongue across her lower lip. Still, no harm in checking. He slipped his hand under the wisp of fabric covering her pussy and tested her wetness.

She was soaked, hot and wet, grinding against his hand.

"You want me to finger fuck you?"

She nodded, gnawing on her lip as she thrust her hips forward.

"I think not. Not quite yet. You'd come in moments, and you know you have to earn that."

"Please, Sir…" Her tone was ragged, her desperation mounting.

"First you have to please me. I have more for you yet."

"What? What more…?"

"This." He bent to pick up the tawse and drew the rigid handle across her shoulder. "Do you know what it is?"

She shook her head.

Tony held the leather under her nose. "Sniff it. Breathe it in. Now do you know?"

"A... a whip, Sir?"

"Almost. Try again."

"Your belt? It's leather."

"It is. You're close. One more try, then I'll show you what this little beauty can do."

"A strap? A spanking crop?"

"That was two tries. Cheating, my little pain slut. You do need a demonstration, don't you?"

"Yes Sir. Anything. Just—please, do it now."

"Oh no, that's not how this works, is it? I decide what happens, and when. You just wait until I'm ready."

"I apologise, Sir." She allowed her head to droop, her distress obvious at having earned a rebuke.

Tony wasn't having that. He cupped her chin to raise her face towards his, and laid his lips across hers. The kiss was gentle, just the merest brush of his mouth at first. Her lips parted and he dipped his tongue inside, stroking her inner cheeks, her teeth, tangling his tongue with hers. He shifted in closer, his chest pressed against her clamped nipples. She winced, he caught the sharp intake of breath, but didn't break the kiss or soften the contact. He knew she needed this, craved the extreme of it. The rush of endorphins would calm and ground her, the euphoria when she came and the subsequent deep sleep he knew would follow would replenish her. His beautiful Thea might be bruised and sore tomorrow, but she'd be purring like a kitten.

At last he lifted his head. Her lips were swollen, pink from his kiss. He kissed her forehead for good measure, and moved around to stand behind her.

He swung the tawse and landed it hard across both buttocks. Thea cried out, her body jerking forward. He waited for several moments, watching the vivid red stripe bloom across her skin, then he shifted to deliver the next stroke. Thea shrieked, dancing on the ring which held her suspended. Tony gauged her response. Thea was an experienced submissive, but the tawse was a harsh instrument. He would check after every stroke, and stop when he believed she'd had enough, whatever she might have to say about that.

He positioned himself for the next stroke and delivered it with absolute precision, just parallel to the first two, on the spot where her bum and thighs met. That had to hurt, she would be sore for days. One more, perhaps two. He raised his arm—

A bright flash halted his stroke in mid air. He whirled, angry.

"What the…"

"Tony, what is it?" Thea was thrashing her head from side to side, unable to see what had disturbed his concentration, but aware that something was amiss. He went straight to her, his arms around her calming her instantly.

"Nothing, sweetheart. Someone messing about, that's all."

"What did they do? I didn't hear anything."

She hadn't seen the flash, the blindfold took care of that. She had no idea that someone had just used a camera in here, a cardinal sin, flouting all the club rules. As he wrapped her in his arms, his instinct to protect kicked into overdrive, Tony watched over her shoulder as two dungeon masters descended on a group of members across the room. There was a lot of head-shaking, angry gesturing, the murmur of voices though nothing more than that. The two members of staff appeared satisfied and returned to their stations at opposite ends of the dungeon.

"Sir?"

Tony brought himself back into the moment fast. Thea still needed him, demanded his entire concentration. He had a scene to conclude, a sub to care for. Anything else would have to wait.

"Two more strokes. Hard ones. Then we stop. Yes?"

"Yes please, Sir."

Yes please! She never failed to delight him. Tony returned to his position behind her, the tawse dangling from his hand. He raised the implement and brought it down hard on her right buttock, leaving a diagonal stripe across the others already there.

Thea's scream reverberated around the room, attracting the attention of both dungeon masters and most of their fellow members. He was aware they'd drawn an audience as he eyed her quivering left buttock, picking his spot.

The tawse whistled through the air, and Thea's cry when it sliced across her skin was nothing short of blood-curdling. It was followed by a series of little yelps as she processed the sensation, her body absorbing the punishment.
Enough.
Tony grabbed the blanket he had folded beside his bag and tossed that over his shoulder. He reached above Thea to release her wrists, and caught her as her legs buckled. In seconds she was enveloped in the blanket and he sank to the floor with her in his arms.
"Okay baby, I have you. Just take a moment. Let me take these off." He tugged at the knot at the back of her head and the scarf fell away. She blinked at him, her expression startled but happy. Next he opened the blanket to reveal her still clamped nipples. It was the work of a moment to loosen the screws and slip the rings off, but he knew it would hurt her. Sure enough, she sobbed as the blood flow was restored. Tony rubbed both nipples hard to help speed the process along. But still, afterwards, she lay shivering in his arms.
"Are you cold?"
"No Sir. Just…"
"You want your orgasm? Is that it?"
"Have I earned it?" Her tone was hopeful.
He chuckled and kissed the top of her head. "I'd say so. I reserved a private recovery room."
"Thank you, Sir."
The rules about nudity were less rigid outside the main dungeon, and non-existent in the private areas. Tony wanted his sub naked for this. He stood and helped Thea to her feet too, steadying her when her legs threatened to give out again. He was quick about collecting up his kit and slinging his bag over his shoulder, then scooped her into his arms again.
As they entered the recovery room he was pleased to see they had the place to themselves. He deposited Thea on one of the long couches and knelt on the floor beside her.
"I'll get you a drink." He helped himself from the fridge full of bottles of water provided for members' use and unsnapped the top from

one of them. He held it to Thea's lips. She sucked at it, swallowing greedily.

When she'd had enough he emptied the remainder of the bottle down his own throat. He swept her hair from her face with his hand, tucking it behind her ear. "Do you want anything else? Apart from a rocking orgasm?"

"Do you have chocolate?"

"Is the Pope a catholic?" He peered into his bag, and produced a pack of chocolate digestive biscuits. He handed one to Thea and waited until she munched her way through it. "Another?"

She nodded, so he handed her the packet. Far be it from him to come between a sated sub and her sugar rush.

Thea made short work of another three biscuits, then offered him the pack. He took it from her and placed it on the floor. "If you want another just say so. Now, I'll be having that thong please."

She wriggled out of the blanket and lifted her bum up to slip the thong down her legs. Tony took it from her and that too found its way into his holdall.

Tony could have instructed her regarding the position he wanted her to adopt, but instead he arranged her himself. She was utterly compliant as he lifted her knees up and pushed them wide, opening and exposing her smooth pussy. Her labia were glistening, slick with her juices. Her clit peeped out from under the hood which partly covered it, and he swore it was becoming plumper before his eyes. Her arousal was obvious, blatant, her need approaching desperate. He took her clit in his mouth and sucked hard.

"Oh, God. Oh, Sir..."

He eased three fingers into her entrance, and pushed them deep. Her pussy was already contracting around his hand, spasming as she succumbed to the climax which had been gathering force as he tormented her in the dungeon. He wouldn't make her wait this time. He wanted her to experience the release, the total abandonment of just letting go.

Moments later, her orgasm engulfed her. She went rigid, her face contorting as he sunk his fingers into her drooling pussy and rubbed her G-spot. He never let up the pressure on her clit, adding his tongue and teeth to the mix as he pleasured her, coaxing every last tremble and shiver and ripple of ecstasy from her.

Only when her body was finally still, her muscles relaxed, her limbs boneless, did he snap open a condom, sheath himself, and drive his cock into her. She wrapped herself around him, clinging to him, her legs around his waist, her ankles crossed in the small of his back. She gripped his shoulders, her face buried against his chest as he rocked his hips slowly. He'd done the hard, intense stuff for this evening, now he just wanted to make love to her.

"Sir, I love you. I love my collar." She moaned the words, muffled in his shirt. He heard her though.

"I love you too, little sub. My slut. My own beautiful whore."

He thrust harder, deeper, the head of his cock nudging her cervix as he buried himself as deep as he could get inside her. His balls tightened, started to contract. Within moments his semen spurted to fill the latex. He held still and let the sensation wash over him.

This was what love felt like, and he was going to get very used to it.

Chapter eleven

Tony ended the call and tossed his phone onto the sofa beside him. He'd received some of the answers he expected, but he remained far from happy. He cocked his head, listening, but heard no sound from upstairs. Thea must still be sleeping. He wasn't surprised, she'd been exhausted when they returned to his house in the small hours of this morning. Their session at the club had been intense, both physically and emotionally. He didn't really expect her to surface until noon, perhaps later still. He'd let her sleep. She needed it.

He sipped his coffee and contemplated the explanation he'd extracted from Jerome, the owner of The Wicked Club. Tony was well aware that the dungeon staff would have reported the flash photography incident, and there would be some sort of investigation. There had to be, the club's membership would demand it. Discretion and privacy were watchwords in the BDSM community and any club unable to guarantee those would be out of business in no time.

Jerome had assured him that Wicked took security seriously, and there would be no repetition of the problem. New signage was even now being displayed, and all members would receive an email by the end of the day reminding them of the absolute ban on taking pictures within the establishment or anywhere in the vicinity. Any member who disregarded this rule could expect to have their membership revoked. The club did reserve the right to conduct random bag searches, and would exercise that right with increased vigilance. Jerome had dismissed the incident as some idiot taking a selfie. A number of guest members had been present the previous evening, and one of them had failed to properly comprehend the regulations regarding use of phones. It was amazing how many people thought selfies didn't count, but the revised signage and the email to members would set them straight. The guest involved had been identified and warned. Jerome had had his assurance that the picture had been deleted. He was confident the matter had been addressed and no further action would be required. He hoped this unfortunate episode would not affect Tony's continued enjoyment of the facilities.

Tony rather thought it might. He was not convinced by the explanation, nor did he really believe that anyone would be so naive as to disregard the no photographs rule. Adequate signage was already in place, the rules were made clear to all guests as they signed in. *Selfies don't count? Whoever heard such bollocks?* Had the phone been checked? No. They only seemed to have this idiot's word for it that the picture had been deleted. He would never have left it at that, not if he'd been in charge.

But he'd had other priorities last night, namely a confused and distressed submissive whose care was his primary concern, then and now. Should he tell her what had happened?

Probably not. She'd be distraught at the possible implications, and would be imagining all sorts of nightmare scenarios. Images posted on social media, blackmail threats, he groaned at the prospect. Thea adored her kink, but she'd probably never go near a club again if she knew about this. Still, it rankled. He was being less than honest with her and that didn't sit well.

*****

"I did what you wanted."

At Tony's words Thea glanced across the office at him, her attention dragged from the third incarnation of the risk assessment policy she was trying to draft. Sometime these things just flowed for her, others, like this one, were squeezed out like blood from a stone. She was glad of the break. Risk management was not the most riveting subject, even on a good day, and she'd be at it all afternoon. Still, she had an entertaining evening to look forward to, with luck. She intended to stay at Tony's again tonight, even though she was due at Kershaw's in the morning.

She removed her glasses and peered at him. "Sorry, what?"

"I did as you suggested. I went to see Jeremy Malone."

"*You* went to see him?"

Tony nodded. "I did. He took some convincing to even agree to that, but I can be persuasive."

"True, you can. But I didn't expect *you* to go. I would have done it."
"I know. You said. But it was my responsibility. And I wanted to find out for myself what sort of bloke he really was."
"And?"
"And you got it right. As usual."
She let that remark pass, resisted the urge to preen. No one likes *I told you so*. "How was he?"
"In what sense?"
"I mean, is he all right? Has he found another job?"
Tony shook his head. "No, It seems the taint of a tribunal isn't easy to shake off. He reckons that any potential employer will perceive him as a trouble-maker, no smoke without fire, that sort of thing. Even though Mr Malone won his case, and was shown to be the injured party, he's been out of work since he left here, almost eight months now."
Thea abandoned any thought of risk assessment. Tony had her full attention. "That's a pity. So, tell me about the visit. Did you go to his home?"
"Yes. I phoned first, and he told me to fuck off. Oh, not in so many words, but that's what it amounted to."
"You can't really blame him."
"No, I thought so too. So I persevered and managed to convince him there'd be no harm in sparing me a few minutes of his time. I offered to meet him at Costa in Millennium Square but he preferred to be on his home turf. So I went there."
"He lives in Morley, right?"
"Yeah, a bungalow. It's just him most of the time, and his daughter at weekends, like you said."
"She wasn't there, then?"
"No."
"I wonder if he gets lonely, now that he doesn't have his job…?"
"Perhaps, though he does some volunteering thing, helping to drag bikes and shopping trolleys out of the River Aire." He paused, met her gaze. "He's a nice guy, Thea. We screwed up, big style."
She'd already known that, in her heart, but even so she was pleased to hear it confirmed.

"Right. So, if you'd known the full story, and if this had happened after you took over Dart Logistics, obviously, how would it have been handled? What would we do differently?"

"We'd have changed his working hours, gone for a more flexible arrangement. He could have had his Monday mornings and Friday afternoons off, and just added a couple of hours to the other working days to make it up. Informally, that's what he did anyway. He generally worked until six thirty or seven from Monday to Thursday, because on those days he would be going home to an empty house, and he was happy to come in early when needed. He could have changed Melanie's transport times, but when he asked they told him that would mean dropping her off on Saturday morning and she'd have to return to her residential school on Sunday afternoon. Neither of them wanted that, they saw little enough of each other as it was."

"Well, that sounds reasonable. But why didn't he tell anyone at work that was what he was doing? What about his time sheets?"

"If Eric's team back then had cross-referenced Jerry's absentee record with his time sheets the truth might well have emerged. No one did though."

Jerry? Interesting. "That was a fundamental error."

Tony's grin was rueful. "Yeah, even I can see that."

"But Mr Malone could have told someone. He could have explained what his problem was, and the solution he'd come up with."

"Yeah, I asked him about that. Seems he was being treated for depression at the time. He told me he just lost interest in everything during those final few months, let it all wash over him and took a fatalistic view. Dart would do what they wanted anyway, and so on. He expected to get fired, and when it happened he just went quietly."

"He didn't stay quiet though."

"No. Like I said, his depression was being treated. He got better. And when he came out of the fog as he tells it, he realised he'd been the victim of a massive injustice, and he wasn't having it. He got some advice—better late than never—and put in his claim for wrongful dismissal. Even then though he didn't base his case on his circumstances, but on the process. He was able to prove that he hadn't been offered a union rep or colleague because those were not mentioned in the letters he had from us. That's in violation of our written disciplinary policy, and the tribunal had an easy time coming to the conclusion we didn't follow our own rules. He was told he'd be onto a sure thing with that, so why bother with the less certain, and much more painful route of laying his personal life in front of the tribunal and hoping they'd sympathise?"

"Makes sense, I suppose."

Tony nodded. "I thought so. And it worked. He got paid out."

"But if he's been out of work for eight months already he can't have much left."

"The twenty five grand amounted to about a year's salary after tax, maybe a little more. He's been living off that, and he's made some economies so he can manage another six months or so before he runs out of savings. Then he'll have to sign on. And things could get tricky. The council might not agree to pay for Melanie's residential school, for example. She's doing well where she is, which is why he kept her there even though he's now at home all day and she doesn't need a residential place."

Thea levelled a shrewd look at him. "You offered to pay for the school, didn't you?"

He returned her gaze. "That was one option, yes."

"And the other options?"

"There was only one other option really, apart from doing nothing. That he return to work, in his old job but on a revised contract."

She lifted one eyebrow, and waited.

"He starts a week on Monday."

Thea let out a squeal which would have been more suited to their dining room, and leapt across the room at him. She threw her arms around his neck and kissed him on the mouth. Hard.

When she allowed him up for air Tony chuckled. "Mrs Richmond, I'm shocked. Is this any way to carry on in the workplace? What do our policies on sexual harassment have to say on the matter? Maybe you need to write us a new one."

"I was sure you'd sort it once you knew. I love you." She kissed him again, this time plunging her tongue into his mouth and taking her time as he returned the kiss. She managed to crawl into his lap, her shoes kicked under his desk. Tony found no further objections to offer

The sound of a throat clearing interrupted the continuation of their 'business meeting'. They both turned. Isabel was framed in the doorway.

Thea thought the PA's expression could best be described as glacial. Self-conscious, but interestingly not nearly as embarrassed as she might once have been to be caught in such a compromising position, she clambered from Tony's lap. She tried not to make too much of a production out of straightening her skirt and offered up thanks that they had not had a few more seconds alone. Who knew what she might have got up to on her Dom's knee? She shuffled around trying to locate her shoes, but despite her efforts Tony had to retrieve one of them for her.

Tony met the interruption with considerably more aplomb. Thea was impressed. She hoped Isabel had not been treated to such displays before between Tony and his senior staff, but somehow she doubted it.

Tony was all smiles. "Isabel, we have good news."

His PA lifted her chin and sniffed, her disapproval almost palpable. "I gathered that much. Am I to understand that congratulations are in order?"

"What? No. Well, yes. Jeremy Malone's coming back. We'll be needing a revised contract for him. Could you run one off please? Mrs Richmond will provide the details of the changes."

Isabel stiffened still more, glaring at the pair of them down her nose. Thea couldn't recall ever seeing the loyal and usually so easy-going PA appear so disgruntled. Her next words were delivered with icy disdain. "I don't think that's a good idea, Tony. I explained that to you already, at the meeting last week. I suggest we all just consider this matter a little further before rushing into any decisions."

Thea was astonished. She was head of corporate services here, and Tony owned the bloody company. They had the right to 'rush into decisions' if they so chose and neither of them required Isabel Barnard's approval. Nor had they asked for it. She opened her mouth to point out something along those lines, but Tony was there ahead of her.

"I know you did, and I appreciate your input, as ever. But this matter is decided, Thea and I both believe this is the correct approach to take. Please make the necessary arrangements with Denise, if you don't mind."

Isabel was not giving up. "But, what about the money we paid him? Even if we did treat him badly, and that's a matter of opinion, he's been compensated."

That question had occurred to Thea and would have been among the next items she intended to raise with Tony. When she remembered.

Tony was unruffled. "Mr Malone wondered about that too. He offered to repay the funds he still has, but I declined. He was the wronged party, his life has been turned upside down by this, and he deserves to keep the money."

Good answer. Thea approved. Isabel apparently did not.

"But, that's just ridiculous!"

"Thank you, Isabel, That'll be all." Tony's voice shifted in an instant to the cool, businesslike tone Thea knew he normally reserved for the bank manager. And for her, but only when she was bound and naked in his dining room.

"But—"

"And would you mind closing the door on your way out please? Thea and I have a number of other matters to discuss."

There followed several moments of awkward, tense silence as Isabel scowled at them both. Her mouth was working but no sound emerged. From the corner of her eye Thea caught the slight movement as Tony tilted his chin in the direction of the door. It was enough, Isabel got the hint. She whirled on her heel and marched back into her outer office, slamming the door behind her.

Thea sat down at her desk again, and looked to Tony for some reaction. Any reaction. Would he even now reconsider based on Isabel's advice?

He grinned at her and rested his chin on his hand. He seemed unaffected by the little altercation, whereas Thea was shaking. She wasn't sure which had disturbed her more—Isabel walking in on their private moment and her undisguised disapproval, or the woman's obvious hostility and anger at the reinstatement of Jeremy

Malone. She saw the working relationship between herself and Isabel disappearing down the toilet. Fast.

"Well," she observed at last, "we could have handled that a bit better."

Tony lifted one expressive eyebrow. "Really? I doubt that somehow."

Isabel may have been dismayed at Tony's about turn in the matter of Jeremy Malone, but Denise Metcalfe was delighted when she heard the news. "Excellent, I'm so pleased we've arrived at an amicable solution. It will boost staff morale to no end."

"But is it workable?" Thea wasn't so sure, and although she applauded Tony's decision in principle, the practical ramifications needed to be ironed out. "Tony offered Mr Malone his old job back. Is that post vacant?"

"Not exactly, but we do have another team leader vacancy in dispatch. Or we will, once the police have charged Shirley Reece with fraud."

"Right, criminal charges would be deemed to justify a finding of gross misconduct, and therefore grounds for instant dismissal from the company with no further investigation required by us. Good thinking. And the contractual revisions?"

"Not a problem. In fact, we could just appoint Mr Malone on the flexitime arrangement you've been developing. It could be a pilot."

Thea stopped to consider that suggestion. She'd been intending to introduce the new, family-friendly working arrangements over the coming months, and might as well start now. "Okay, do it that way then. Give me a shout if you need anything else from me."

She ended the call and started to log off from her computer. It had been a long day and she was keen to find Tony and head for home. As though summoned by her thoughts his voice reached her from the outer office.

"Thea and I will be leaving soon. If Mr Peters from our accountants' rings could you make an appointment in Thea's diary for him? Next Tuesday or Friday should be fine."

Thea couldn't make out the mumbled reply, but she was reasonably certain that even though it had been a few hours ago Isabel would still be smarting from the earlier confrontation. Still, that was her problem.

"Ready for the off?" Tony entered the office, and she was struck, not for the first time, by the way he seemed to fill the space. He was a formidable presence, as Isabel had learnt this afternoon, when she crossed him.

Thea signalled for Tony to close the door, and when she was sure they wouldn't be overheard she asked if Isabel was alright.

"Not really. She's sulking."

"Have you ever had a row like that with her before? You always seem to get on so well."

He shook his head. "We don't always agree, that goes without saying. But she's never gone up against me so directly before. Or been so bloody condescending. She spoke to us like we were a couple of naughty children, for fuck's sake. I encourage people to say what they think, and I do listen. But I won't put up with that."

"No. Right. But she was probably surprised to see us… well, you know."

"I get that. But we're consenting adults, and this is my office. Yours too, for the duration. She'll have to get used to it."

"Even so, I'll be a little less demonstrative next time you make a decision I agree with."

"Well, that'd be a pity, but I suppose it's your call. I, on the other hand, will have no compunction at all about instructing you to strip and kneel, if the occasion demands it. Though not in front of Isabel if we can help it of course."

Thea grinned, her pussy clenching. She wanted to be at home. Quick. "So, is she still out there?" She did not relish the prospect of any further confrontation tonight.

"Coward. She was just putting her coat on. We'll give her a couple of minutes, until the coast's clear."

"Are you avoiding her too, Mr diMarco?"

"I pick my battles, Mrs Richmond. And like you, I've had enough of them for today."

"Right. A couple of minutes then."

The sound of the door from Isabel's office to the main corridor opening, then closing, was Thea's signal to grab her coat. They were just about to leave when they heard the outer door opening again, this time more forcefully.
"Shit! Is she back?" Tony dumped his briefcase back on the desk and waited.
There was a loud knock on their office door.
"Come in." They both called out together.
A breathless and distinctly flustered Eric Henderson bustled into the room. His overcoat was unbuttoned, flapping around his legs. He'd clearly been running. He clutched several crumpled sheets of paper in his hand.
"Eric, are you all right?" Tony pulled out Thea's abandoned chair and gestured the man to sit. Eric did so, fanning himself with the papers he still grasped.
"I'll get him a drink of water." Thea headed for the dispenser in the corridor and returned a few moments later, a plastic cup of chilled water at the ready. Eric was no less dishevelled and agitated, but by now Tony's face was ashen too. He held one of the Eric's sheets of paper in his hand, smoothed out somewhat, and was glaring at it. Thea halted in the doorway, taking in the scene. Something was wrong. Very wrong.
"Tony...?"
He looked at her. She had never seen him so angry.
"Sir..?"
He shook his head, turned away.
"It's a forgery. Some sort of Photoshop thing. It must be..." Eric sounded bemused.
Tony's reply was low, his voice little more than a growl. "The picture is genuine."
"But, I don't understand. It looks like you and..." Eric turned to face Thea, his expression one of shock, disbelief. But she detected sympathy there too.
"What's happened? What looks like us?" She came into the room and placed the paper cup on her desk, staring from one man to the other.

"She needs to see it. She'll see soon enough." This from Eric, who appeared to be regaining his composure slightly.

"See what? What, Tony? What's happened?" A solid lump of fear settled in the pit of Thea's stomach. She stepped forward, approaching Tony. Surely he wasn't angry with her? What had she done? She reached for him, placed her hand on his elbow.

He didn't turn around, but neither did he shake off her touch. His tone was clipped as he spoke over his shoulder to his head of IT.

"Eric, where did you find this?"

"In the car park. I was just leaving, and I spotted it tucked under my windscreen wiper. All the cars still there had them. I went round and gathered up the ones I could see, and brought them all here. I thought you'd better see it, straight away. But there'll be others, people who left earlier..."

Tony nodded, and turned to face Thea. He reached for her and enfolded her in a hug. She was nearly faint with relief. He wasn't angry with her then. But in that case, what?

"I'm sorry, sweetheart. I should have seen this coming, prevented it somehow." His voice was harsh, but she knew his displeasure was not directed at her.

"Seen what? Prevented what? Tony, you're not making sense."

"Are you two...? I mean, is this...?" Eric sounded baffled. Thea reflected that he was not the only one.

"A forgery? No."

"I...see." From his tone it was apparent that Eric didn't see at all, but Thea directed her attention to Tony.

"Please, tell me what's going on. What picture?"

Tony groaned, his arms loosened to release her. "This one, love." He handed her the sheet of paper.

Thea gazed at it, disbelief washing over her, followed by revulsion. She might be sick. Correction, she was going to throw up. Now.

"Christ! Oh Jesus, how did this...? I mean, who..." She broke off to make a dash for the private loo in the corner of Tony's office, where she deposited the remains of her lunch in the toilet. She flushed, rinsed her face, and finally emerged to find just Tony waiting for her. He was seated at his desk, the sheet of paper spread out in front of him. She averted her eyes from the image, grainy, photocopied, but unmistakable.

Her body, suspended from the ceiling in The Wicked Club dungeon, blindfolded and as near to naked as made no real difference. Tony was standing beside her in the picture, his whip hand raised, the tawse caught in sharp focus, its motion suspended in the air. Thea's shoulders and buttocks were clearly visible and displayed the distinct marks of the whipping she had enjoyed, continued to enjoy if her near ecstatic expression was any indication. Which of course it was.

"Where's Eric?" She started with the inconsequential. It gave her time to think.

"I sent him home."

"I see."

"He won't discuss this."

"What does it matter? I suppose everyone's seen that picture now." She stood before Tony's desk, her body shaking.

"We don't know how many staff returned to their cars before Eric left, but yes, it's safe to assume it's out there."

Thea nodded, grateful at least that he made no attempt to dismiss the enormity of what had happened. At least she was spared that.

"I don't understand. Where did this picture come from? It's us, the other night, isn't it?"

It was Tony's turn to nod.

"But, how? Surely someone would have seen. The rules say no cameras. No one takes pictures." She peered at him, hopeless. Despite her words, her disbelief, the reality of the situation was apparent. Someone had taken the picture, and what's more they seemed intent on using it to humiliate both of them. Except, Tony didn't seem to care. At least, not for himself. And although he was shocked, and angry, through her haze of confused despair one fact emerged clear, strong, and utterly astonishing. He didn't appear surprised.

"You knew. You knew about this, didn't you?"

He met her gaze, held it. Then he nodded again. "I suspected it, yes. I knew it was a possibility."

"How? How did you know?"

"I saw the camera flash. While you were blindfolded."

Thea doubled up as another wave of nausea washed through her. "Oh God, why didn't you tell me. If you knew…?"

"I saw the flash, but not who took the picture. I was concentrating on you at the time. I didn't know what they took a picture of either. None of us did. We all saw the flash, and the dungeon staff did ask around. Not much, I know, but short of body searching everyone there I guess they did what they could."

"They should have stopped it. Found the camera. They had no right…"

Tony stood and rounded the desk to enfold her in his arms again. "I know. Fuck, I know that. I spoke to the club owner afterwards, but it was too late by then. He told me that they had identified the culprit, and that the picture was a selfie. He also told me it had been deleted. They took his word for it. Clearly, they shouldn't have. I'm sorry. You don't deserve this. I wish I could have protected you."

"But, why us? And what's all this about anyway? These photocopies…?" She shoved at his chest to stand back, and looked up at him, alarmed. "Someone must have known who we were. Why else are those images here? In our car park? Oh God, they stuck that picture under every windscreen wiper. All our staff…"

Tony's mouth flattened in a sympathetic grimace. "Seems like it."

"It was targeted. At us. But why?"

"I don't know. I intend to find out though."

"How? And why bother? The damage is done now. Oh Christ, I can't work here any more."

"Sweetheart, you can. You have to. You can't just give in. That's what they want."

"What about what I want. My privacy? I knew I should never have let you mix it all up. This would never have happened if you hadn't confused me, made me let down my guard." In a sudden and overwhelming rush of violent anger Thea aimed her clenched fist at his chest. It connected and bounced off, useless. Impotent. Like her, like her rage. She struck out again, this time landing a punch to his jaw. His head tilted back, but he seemed oblivious to her attempts to do him grievous harm. That just fuelled her anger.

Thea screamed and laid into him, raining ferocious blows on his chest, his shoulders, his arms. Tony allowed it, absorbed her assault, waited until her temper and frustration were spent before wrapping his arms around her again.

"I know, love. I know. We'll get to the bottom of this, I promise you that."

"But what good will it do? We'll never live this down. Everyone knows. Everything's ruined."

"Not ruined. We're pissed off. And embarrassed maybe, but that'll pass. There'll be talk, a lot of talk for a few days, then everyone will move on."

"They won't. It'll never pass. I can't face anyone again after this. Neither can you."

"I'll survive. So will you. Nothing we've done is illegal, and if anyone thinks it's immoral then that's a matter of opinion. People here will be surprised, amused. Some might even be offended but if they want to hang on to their jobs they'll keep that view to themselves. This *will* blow over, Thea."

She shook her head, her knees weak now that her violent tantrum was over. She wanted to sit down. Better still lie down. In the dark. The doors locked. She needed to hide.

"I want to go home."

"Of course. Let's get out of here."

"No. My home. I want to go to my flat."

"Okay." Tony sounded less enthusiastic at that, but ready to do it her way.

"No. On my own. Just me."

"I don't think that's a good idea."

Another brief flash of anger flared within her. "Oh, and you're such a great judge of what constitutes a good idea. I was fine until I started doing things your way."

"Now Thea…"

His warning tone was lost on her. She whirled away from him, grabbing her coat from her desk where she'd deposited it when Eric first hurtled into the room a lifetime ago. She shouldered her bag and headed for the door.

"Thea! Wait."

"Fuck off. This is all your fault."

That's no way to talk to your Dom. The thought flittered uselessly among the tangle of emotions coursing through her as she slammed the door behind her.

Chapter twelve

"What have you been up to? I agreed to let you borrow Mrs Richmond, not whip her half to death."

Tony groaned at hearing the familiar voice, on this occasion laced with a liberal dash of disapproval. "Hello Stephen."

"Don't hello me, lad. What's been going on?"

"You know about our little problem then?" Tony had learnt long ago not to even think about hedging with his godfather.

"Some joker sent me a picture. To my home at that. What if Diana had seen it?"

Privately Tony thought Stephen's wife was made of sterner stuff than her husband gave her credit for and would have likely survived the shock, but he didn't share that opinion. He settled back on the sofa in his dining room, an untouched glass of whisky on the low table in front of him, and resigned himself to a difficult conversation.

"But she didn't. Has Thea been in touch with you?"

"No. Does she know about this then? The picture I mean, not the, the…"

"Yes, she knows."

"Shit! How did she take it?"

"Not well."

"I'm not bloody surprised. For crying out loud, what is this? I mean, what were you playing at?"

"Isn't that obvious?" Tony failed to conceal the exasperation in his voice. It didn't go down well.

"Don't take that tone with me lad. I know it's glaringly bloody obvious what you were up to. What I want to know is, why did you let someone take a photo of the pair of you? And then send copies to all and sundry? What you do for fun is your own concern, behind closed doors. That goes for Thea too. But couldn't you have been a bit more discreet?"

"It's a long story, Stephen."

"And it's not a story I particularly want to hear. Christ, Thea must be mortified. Is she there?"

"No. She went home."

"And you just let her? On her own?"

"It wasn't my preferred option, admitted."
"So why? If you're into all this, this control stuff, how come you didn't stop her?"
Good question. "It's not that simple…"
"It's every bit that simple. I'm going over there. She shouldn't be alone right now. She needs to know who her friends are."
Tony couldn't argue with that. Neither was it lost on him that Thea appeared to be the exclusive object of his godfather's sympathy. Whatever, he wasn't about to let Stephen Kershaw take over his responsibilities.
"No need. I'll go." He realised he'd been planning to anyway, which explained why his whisky remained untouched after almost two hours
"You do what you like, lad. I'm going to see her. Now."
"I'll meet you over there then."
The phone clicked as Stephen hung up. Tony had the distinct impression he'd just been manipulated.

He heard the banging even before he entered the converted mill where Thea had an apartment on the second floor. He could hear the din from outside. And above that Stephen's voice, raised, demanding entry.
"Thea! I know you're in there. It's me. Let me in." More thunderous knocking, then. "Thea! If I have to get a sledgehammer, I will. Open the bloody door."
Tony jogged up the two flights of stairs to join Stephen on the landing on Thea's floor. The older man raised his fist and hammered again on the solid wood.
"Here. Let me." Tony tapped him on the shoulder.
Stephen rounded on him. "I can thump a door as well as you can." His expression suggested he might not stop at attacking the door.
"I don't doubt it. Neither do any of Thea's neighbours. Maybe it's time for a more subtle approach though."
"Right. If you've got a better idea feel free, bright spark."
Tony fished a key out of his trouser pocket. "I'll start with this."
Stephen grunted and stepped aside. Tony slipped the key in the lock and opened the door.

The hallway was in darkness, the place silent.
"I thought you said she'd be here."
"She is. Or she should be. She told me she wanted to come home, alone." Tony advanced along the hallway. He hit the light switch and started opening doors. He hadn't been here more than a couple of times, they preferred his house. It was bigger, more possibilities. Still, he remembered the layout and quickly eliminated the kitchen and living room. That only left the bathroom, which was off her bedroom. He opened the bedroom door and his heart stopped for a few seconds as he took in the scene.
The bottle of pills, opened on the bedside table, its contents scattered across the carpet beside the bed. A wet stain on the wall opposite the door, the shattered remains of what looked to be a wine glass on the floor. And in the bed, the shape of her body concealed under the duvet, lay Thea. Still, so still.
"Christ! Fucking hell, Stephen, call an ambulance." Tony hurled himself across the room and ripped the duvet from the inert form on the bed. Stephen was right on his heels, digging in his pocket for his phone.
"What's happened? What has she done?" The older man was dialling nine nine nine as he spoke, but Tony assumed the question was rhetorical anyway. He grabbed Thea and pulled her into a sitting position. She was fully dressed, apart from her shoes. She still had her coat on, the same one she had grabbed as she fled from their office earlier that day. Tony gave her a quick shake. "Thea, speak to me. Thea!"
Her eyes were closed, and remained so, though he felt rather than saw the shudder which ran through her. She seemed to be conscious, trying to shake off Tony's grip.
"Ambulance please. Overdose I think." Stephen's tone was crisp and business-like. Tony admired his ability to respond to the emergency before emotions could get in the way. He was glad the older man was here because he was not at all sure he'd cope alone.
"No. No ambulance." Thea murmured the words, but they were clear, sharp.
Tony tipped her chin up with his fingers. "Thea, look at me. Are you okay? Did you take any?"

"What?"

"How many did you take?"

"How many what? Leave me alone."

She was starting to struggle in earnest, but Tony tightened his grip.

"Pills, for fuck's sake. How many did you take?"

"What pills? What are you talking about?"

"These fucking pills." Tony grabbed the half empty bottle and rattled the remaining contents in front of her face. "Was this full?"

"What? Yes. No... I spilled them."

"I can see that. How many have you taken though?" He was struggling to remain calm, as calm as Stephen who was talking to the emergency operator, giving directions to Thea's apartment. Despite his efforts Tony's voice was rising as desperation started to take hold. He couldn't lose her, not like this. Not now.

Thea tried again to shake off his hold but without success. "Are you mad? I told you, I spilled them."

"How many, Thea? How many pills did you take?"

"None. I didn't take any because I spilt them and I couldn't be bothered picking them up. Happy now?"

Tony stared at her, a flicker of hope flaring. "Are you sure?"

"Do I look like an idiot to you? Really? Of course I'm bloody sure."

"None?"

"None."

"So why's the bottle here? It isn't usually."

Thea gave up struggling and lay back against the pillows, her eyelids drooping. "It is, actually. But I normally keep them in the drawer. My head was spinning when I came in, churning. I wanted to sleep so I intended to take one, two perhaps. But my hands were shaking and I dropped the lot. It was just too much bother to get out of bed and start gathering them back up so I left them. I'll sort it. Later."

"And the broken glass?"

"A moment of anger. Frustration. I threw it. After I dropped the sleeping pills."

"Sorry, false alarm. No ambulance required after all. Thank you." Stephen ended the call, then moved to stand at the foot of the bed.

"You'd better take her into the living room while I clear this lot up. Don't let her stand on the floor with bare feet."

Thea rolled onto her side, her eyes still closed. "No, I'm staying here. I'll be fine, I just want to be on my own."

"Bollocks. Not happening." Tony slipped an arm under her knees ready to lift her, but Thea wriggled away from him across the bed.

"If I wanted company I'd have answered the bloody door. Can't you two take a hint?" She cracked open her eyes to peer at Stephen, clearly puzzled. "What are you doing here anyway?"

"He got a picture too. Home delivery." Tony hadn't intended the words to be as stark as they sounded, nor his tone so bitter. He put it down to sheer mind-numbing relief that she seemed to be okay. Sort of.

"Oh God!" Thea turned to bury her face in the pillow, sobs racking her body.

Perhaps not okay exactly. Tony abandoned his attempt to lift Thea from the bed in favour of climbing onto the mattress alongside her. He wrapped his arms around her and hung on, even as she tried to shake him loose again. After a few attempts she gave in, turned, and grabbed handfuls of his T shirt in her fists. She clung on, weeping against his chest as Tony caressed her back and shoulders, muttering nonsense into her hair.

For several minutes the only movement in the room was Stephen as he went about the business of clearing up. He picked up each of the white tablets strewn across the carpet and put them back in the bottle, then shoved that into his trouser pocket.

Tony believed Thea's account of what had happened, but even so there was no point tempting fate. He watched as Stephen picked up the largest of the fragments of glass and wrapped them in newspaper before hunting round for Thea's vacuum cleaner. By the time the older man was finished no trace of pills or broken glass remained. Stephen came to sit on the edge of the bed.

"I think we all need a cup of tea, and a chat. I'll see you both out there." He gestured to the living room. "We need to work out who has it in for our Thea here."

"Right. We'll be there in a minute." Tony shifted to cup Thea's face in his hand again. "Are you ready?"

"Not really."

"I know, but we do need to talk. About what happened here, before we arrived. And about what to do next."

"What can we do? It's happened, and…"

"We'll get to that. But first, pills aren't the answer. I need to hear you say that."

"I know that. I just intended to get a few hours' sleep. I'm pissed off, hurt, embarrassed. Humiliated to the core. But suicidal? No."

"You swear."

"Yes. I swear."

"So, what did happen? Why didn't you answer the door? How come you're cowering in your bed with your coat on?" His tone had gentled, but Tony wasn't backing off. He would have this out, here and now. He preferred to deal with it just the two of them, though he would have no compunction about enlisting Stephen if need be.

Thea drew in a long breath, then lifted her gaze to meet his. Her face was ravaged, red and blotched by tears, but he detected the remnants of the brave, determined sub he knew so well. She was coming back to him.

"I got home, and I wandered around the flat for a while. I don't know how long. I never even thought about taking my coat off."

"Go on."

"I was so miserable. It felt—hopeless. And I was ashamed, ashamed of what I'd done. What I was. Am. And that everyone knew."

"I'm letting that remark go for now, because I want to hear this, to understand. But you know what I'm going to say, and do, about that eventually. Don't you?"

"It's different for you. You're so, so—outgoing. You don't care what anyone thinks. I do. I always have."

"You're wrong there. I do care what others think. I just don't let other people's opinions rule my life. I make my own choices, and as long as I harm no one, I have nothing to reproach myself for. Neither do you. What has happened is a gross invasion of your privacy. Our privacy. We're the victims here, we're not the ones in the wrong."

Thea nodded, but without conviction. Tony pressed home his point.

"You feel wounded, damaged. I get that, I do understand. You've been hurt. So have I, but not nearly so much as you. But we *will* get past this. Together. We hold our heads up, and we answer questions if we choose to. Or not. Our choice."

"I'm not sure I can. Hold my head up I mean. Face people."

"You will. I know you will. Even if I have to put a posture collar on you."

"You wouldn't."

"Don't test me on that, little sub. I prefer not to though. I like the collar you have."

As if reminded of her status in his life Thea fingered the delicate gold and leather chain around her neck. "I like it too."

"Still? Even after this you don't want to ask me to remove it?"

"No! No, of course not." Her vehement response provided the comfort and reassurance he had been seeking. She was still his. "Good. So, all this…?"

Thea dropped her gaze, and Tony knew she was already processing what had happened, the implications. She was working her way through it.

"I just wanted some peace. My head was in a mess, I couldn't think straight. I wanted to sleep, I thought things would look better when I woke up. I had the sleeping pills in the drawer. My doctor prescribed them for me a while ago, and I used to take one occasionally. Not for some time now though. You seem to tire me out recently." She managed an embarrassed grin. Tony dropped a kiss on her forehead by way of acknowledgement but didn't want to distract her from her account. Thea continued. "So I came in here, and got into bed. Fully clothed. I suppose I must have got myself a glass of water, though I don't really remember that…"

She glanced down, only now apparently realising she still wore her coat. "Oh God, what was I thinking?" She unbuttoned the coat and took it off, then tossed it at the foot of the bed before continuing her story. "I tried to tip a couple of pills into my hand. But they went everywhere. Then suddenly I was angry. At me, at you, at the bastard who took that photo. It was as though a red mist came down. So I threw the glass at the wall. Then I buried myself under the duvet. I didn't intend to come out. Well, not for a while. I figured that was the next best thing to oblivion."

"Right. I guess we're all entitled to hide once in a while. I don't begrudge you the moment. But eventually you have to come out."

"I wanted to hide for a good long time. Still do. But then there was all that din outside. I recognised Stephen's voice and he was the last person I wanted to see. I pulled the duvet over my head and put my hands over my ears. I thought he'd get fed up, or think I wasn't here and he'd just go away. I can't face him. Please, Tony, can't you just explain…?"

He shook his head. "You *can* face him. He cares about you, and nothing else matters to him as long as you're alright. He's out there now making you a cup of tea. Does that sound like judging to you?"

"No, but…"

"People are going to surprise you, Thea, starting with Stephen. Their reactions to those pictures won't be as you imagine. And if anyone does kick off, we don't have to listen. They can find themselves somewhere else to work, someone else to lecture. Agreed?"

"I don't know…"

"I do. Agreed?" He had a way of talking to her, a tone he reserved for moments like this, when he expected to be obeyed. Intended it. It seemed it was not lost on Thea. She looked up at him again, her expression hardening. "Yes, okay. Agreed. I think."

"Good. We'll practice on Stephen now, and maybe on Diana later, if you feel up to it. And tomorrow, we'll talk to Denise, Eric and Chris. And Isabel."

Thea grimaced. "Tomorrow? So soon? Wouldn't it be better to let the dust settle a bit?

"No. They'll be talking anyway. Speculating. We should take control."

"That's the Dom speaking."

"Maybe, but it doesn't make me wrong. I trust my instincts on this, and I need you to trust me too. You don't usually have a problem with that."

"No Sir, I suppose not. But do we really have to talk to Isabel about this? I know what she'll say."

"After today, I can guess too. But Isabel's not daft and she'll do as she's told. She's my PA. That doesn't give her the right to comment on my private life or relationships. If I have to spell that out to her, I will. She'll see it my way. Well, I hope so. She has two choices."

Thea managed a weak smile. "My gran would call that brazening it out."

"Your gran sounds to have been a wise lady."

"She is. I think you'd like her. I have no idea at all what she'll make of you though."

"Where does she live?"

"Somerset. That's where all my family are."

"We'll be driving down there soon enough, I imagine. I want to meet them."

"I think I'd like that."

Tony smiled, and realised only now that he'd been holding his breath. He shuddered as he privately acknowledged how desperate he'd been when he thought, in those few panicked moments, that he might have lost her. And it would have been his own fault. He should never have let her leave the office on her own. Stephen was right about that much, at least.

And talking of Stephen... "Come on. If we're going to make your gran proud and brazen this out, let's get started." He stood and held out his hand to Thea. She took it and got to her feet.

"So, who have you pissed off, Thea?" Stephen regarded the pair of them under his eyebrows as they sipped tea in Thea's living room. "Me? Why should this vendetta be aimed at me? Surely this is as much about Tony."

Tony shook his head. "I thought so too at first. But my connection with Kershaw's is less well known. Stephen is my godfather, but only my family and close friends would be aware of that. To most he's just a business associate, a friend perhaps. Not enough to justify going round to his house and posting that picture through his letterbox. My hunch is the same as Stephen's, this bastard has it in for you. I'm caught in the crossfire, but the real target is you, Thea.

So why would that be? And more to the point, how did they get that picture?"

"At the club the other night, you said you saw the flash."

"I did. That's not what I mean though. That was when the picture was taken, sure enough. But someone had to have known we were going to be there that night, at The Wicked Club. I'm guessing they paid someone to sign in, probably as a guest, with instructions to take a photo. It'd be good to know who that guest with the camera was, but what we really need to find out is who wanted that picture so much.

"Agreed. But how will we ever find that out?"

"We'll buy the information. If someone was prepared to do this for money, my guess is they'll be happy to tell us who paid them, if we offer more cash. It's worth trying, anyway."

"I'll chip in." Stephen leaned forward, his expression intent. "Whatever that bastard got for the pictures in the first place, we'll double it."

Tony glanced at him. "We don't expect you to pay. I can cover it."

"No way. I've been dragged into this, and I intend to see it sorted. Mrs Richmond is set to take over Kershaw's when I retire, which I hope won't be too long now. I need her back at the helm, in control, on top of things. If I have to pay a few quid, it'll be worth it. Anyway, I want to help nail this malicious creep."

"I never said I'd take over. You can't retire yet." Thea stared at her elderly employer, her eyes widening.

She reminded Tony of a rabbit caught in headlights and he wondered why she was so opposed to this development. It seemed to him a natural progression in her career. She might be a submissive in her relationship with him, but Thea was nothing if not ambitious at work.

"You will. There's no one else. Except him, obviously," Stephen jerked his thumb in Tony's direction, "but he's got too much on already, what with this new company he's taken on. No, it'll have to be you. I've had the papers drawn up."

"What papers? You can't have."

"The contract of sale. You can buy the company from me, at a preferential rate, of course. The bank has already approved the loan in principle, the firm is excellent surety. And don't you look at me like that. You knew I was considering this, talking to the bank and the solicitors."

"Talking, not deciding. It's up to me, not you. And I say no. I'll work with whoever takes over, whether it's Tony or someone else. And I'll help in the transition. But I'm not buying Kershaw's."

Tony had seen Thea agitated often enough. He'd seen her body tremble as he flogged her, and he'd watched her shake with lust as he edged her to the brink of orgasm and held her there, but he'd never seen her so defensive before. It was obvious to him that she could run Kershaw's in her sleep, so what was the big objection? He was curious, but they all had more pressing matters to contend with right now.

"We'll come back to this. First, I need to make a phone call." He tapped a few numbers into his speed dial, and waited for the call to be answered.

"Jerome? Hello, it's Tony diMarco. So, that picture—it wasn't a selfie." He launched straight in, forgoing the usual niceties and any preamble, He'd heard all the bullshit he was going to accept from Jerome and now he wanted answers. Hard facts. He was ready to demand the information he required, and he wouldn't be taking no for an answer.

He paused, listening as Jerome tried again to pass the incident off as something and nothing. Tony had heard enough and broke into the prepared spiel. "I do know it wasn't a fucking selfie, because a photograph of me and my sub has been printed off and distributed around my staff, and to my sub's employer too. This is malicious and I need to know who's behind it." Tony listened again, his patience evaporating as Jerome explained the reasons why he couldn't possibly divulge details of the culprit, and he accepted the absolute promise that this particular guest would not be allowed entry again, in any circumstances. He waited until Jerome had completed his speech, then he returned to his original point, his voice low. "Jerome, you know and I know how small the fetish community is. How tight knit. Within twenty four hours everyone will know what's happened, and the Wicked might as well close down now. The only way you're going to maintain any credibility is to cooperate with me. I want to know who paid for that photo, and I expect you to find that out for me. If you would, please."

Tony tossed a quick smile at his audience of two as Jerome spluttered and protested again, but he knew he was going to have his way. The club owner had no realistic alternative, not if he wanted to save his business.

"Here's how. You'll offer him money. I know you know who took that picture. You told me you spoke to him. So you'll go back to whoever it was and tell them that we know they were paid by someone, and we'll pay them twice as much if they tell us who their customer was. I bet we'll find that this is one greedy little bastard, he'll be ready to sell his grandmother. And Jerome, tell him I want that information within the next hour or there's no deal."

Tony ended the call and leaned back on the sofa, satisfied for the time being.

"What happens now? What did he say?" Thea was gazing at him, her nervousness showing.

"He'll phone me back when he has the information I want. So now, Thea, we wait. And while we're waiting we can discuss your career prospects at Kershaw's. Why don't you want to put old Stephen here out of his misery and take over? Kershaw's is a sound enough investment, and you know the company like the back of your hand."

"It's complicated."

"No, sweetheart, dealing with idiots who put pictures of us under windscreen wipers is complicated. This is just a bit hard to follow. So go on, enlighten me. Enlighten both of us."

"Just leave it. Please."

"No. Now don't get me wrong, if I thought it was what you wanted I'd do everything I could to keep you at Dart indefinitely, but once you've knocked us into shape you'd be bored to tears. You need to be running your own ship, not crewing mine, or his. Buying Kershaw's makes perfect sense."

"I'm not cut out for it, that's all."

"That's not all. That's fucking nonsense. Try again."

Thea hunched at her end of the sofa, and brought her knees up to her chest in a posture Tony considered far too typically defensive for his liking. He let that go for now though and zeroed in on what she had said. "So, what are you cut out for? In your opinion"

"It's not just my opinion. You said it too. Weeks ago, when we talked about bicycles, and pedalling. I'm a pedaller, not a handlebars sort of person."

"What's she on about? What does any of this have to do with bikes for Christ's sake?" Stephen looked beyond bewildered. They both ignored him.

"Right, but didn't I also tell you that no business is a one man show. Or one woman show in your case. You know your strengths, as I know mine. So you need to surround yourself with people you can trust who bring other qualities that you don't have. What is it you'd need to buy in?"

"Everything!"

"No. You can pedal. You do great pedalling. What was that about handlebars?"

"All that stuff you do. And Stephen. The schmoozing, the deals, the chatting to clients. I can run systems, but I can't sell anything to save my life. I can't get new business in. I'd be bankrupt in months and my workers out of a job."

"So you hire yourself a managing director. Someone with marketing flair, leadership. A strategist. Tell them what you want doing and leave them to get on with it while you do what you're good at behind the scenes."

Thea offered him a wry smile. "Are you looking for a job, Tony?"

He stopped, considered her tongue in cheek suggestion for a few moments, then, "Mates rates then. And if I agree to work for you it's on condition that you stay on as my deputy director at Dart. Indefinitely. I won't be able to manage both companies unless you do."

"What?"

"You heard. It's a good solution. You should take up Stephen's offer, buy him out, then hire me to head up your public-facing activity. We know we can work together, we make a great team."

"You mean both of us, run both companies? Like a partnership?"

"We could structure it that way if you like. Let's take some legal advice on it. But yes, that's the general idea. Does it sound like something you'd like to do?"

"I can't imagine myself as your boss."

"I confess that has me a little stymied too. But a partnership might work. You pedal both firms, I deal with all the handlebars stuff. Do we have a deal?"

He held out his hand. Stephen's expression remained one of absolute bewilderment but he seemed to know to keep his mouth shut. Thea took Tony's hand and gave it a firm shake.

"Deal. Partners."

Tony might have made more of an attempt to seal their new arrangement, but he felt the moment was not quite right for what he had in mind. Still…

He abandoned that train of thought when his phone rang. He checked the caller ID. It was Jerome

Chapter thirteen

"No answer." Tony ended the call and slipped his phone back into his trouser pocket.

Thea carried two mugs of tea through from her tiny kitchen and set them down on a low table beside the sofa. Stephen had left already. She wriggled up alongside Tony. "I didn't expect there to be, not really. We wouldn't get that lucky, would we?"

"Who knows? I'll try again later. Are we staying here tonight or do you want to come to mine?"

"We? You don't need to babysit me. I had a shock, and I was upset. More than upset, but I'm fine. Really." Now that she'd regained—or perhaps acquired—a sense of proportion Thea was mortified at how she'd behaved. She'd cowered in her bed like some sort of pathetic loser, as though she could block all her problems out. It wasn't her, not her way of dealing with adversity at all. Thea Richmond was a coper, a problem-solver. And she was tough. She must be, she could weather a session on the receiving end of Tony's belt.

She didn't relish the prospect of what the next few days had to offer. However hard she tried she knew she would never achieve Tony's blasé attitude, and maybe she didn't want to. But she'd get through it, past it, and she could see a future beyond. A bright, glittering future, at work and in her personal life.

She wore Tony's collar, and even if she had managed to lose sight of it briefly, she knew full well the implications of that. He hadn't said so, but she fully expected him to punish her for her idiotic behaviour earlier. And that discipline needed to be imminent. It couldn't wait. *She* couldn't wait. She understood why. She'd behaved irrationally. She'd scared him. Hell, she'd scared herself and she felt so ashamed of it now. She wanted to feel the bite of his belt across her arse, needed it. Craved it. Nothing else would make this right. Her submissive nature was as much a part of her as her ruthless professional efficiency. Somehow she'd managed to not see that, not value that aspect of herself.

Well, no longer. It stopped. Here. Now.

"I need a spanking." Thea's gaze was level as she stood before Tony, her voice low but steady. "Please, Sir."

"I know."

"Will you do it here? Now?" She was hopeful, but anxious too. What if he decided to make her wait, to draw out the agony and the ecstasy of it all? She prayed not, but at the same time Thea feared what the coming few minutes would bring. She was experienced enough to know full well the difference between a punishment spanking and an erotic one. This would hurt. A lot.

Tony narrowed his eyes at her, and her heart sank further. "Yes, here. And soon. But first I want you to set out for me, and for yourself, exactly why you deserve to have your sweet arse blistered." He settled himself in one of her two armchairs, crossing his ankle over his knee as Thea continued to stand, her chin tilted up in a posture she hoped would denote pride rather than defiance. Tony's gaze hardened. "Thea, I'm waiting."

"Yes, Sir, I apologise." She scrambled her thoughts together quickly. "It's several things really. I was very rude to you earlier, at the office. Then I stormed out and came here alone, even though you told me I shouldn't." She paused.

Tony remained immobile, waiting for more. Thea took a deep breath and ploughed on.

"Then I locked myself in, and refused to answer the door. I didn't mean to alarm anyone, but I realise now how it must have seemed..."

Still Tony offered no response, though neither did he take issue with anything she had said so far. Thea lowered her gaze to the floor, making no attempt to check the tears now flowing down her cheeks.

"I forgot what it means to be a collared submissive. *Your* submissive, Sir. You taught me to be proud, but when it mattered I was a coward. I ran away and hid, ashamed of what I am. Who I am."

"And now?"

"I think I have my head together again, Sir."

He gave a slow nod. "I think so too, and that's important. I do realise how shocked and distressed you were. You reacted badly at first, but not any longer. I'm pleased with you, and it's my turn to be proud. That just leaves the discipline you need me to deliver, to ensure you never forget something so fundamental again. I intend to teach you that lesson now, Thea."

"I know Sir, and I am grateful for it. Thank you." She started to sink to her knees.

"Not yet. I want you naked first." His tone was cold, crisp, his expression stern when she chanced a peep at him.

Thea straightened and started to unbutton her blouse. Tony waited, his demeanour patient now, as she removed her clothing. Thea had undressed for him on countless occasions before now, but never had she felt so vulnerable, or so exposed. With each item she folded and placed on the arm of her other chair her stomach churned and her pussy clenched. She was scared. No, scratch that, terrified. But the familiar twist of arousal that always preceded a scene was already causing her pussy to moisten.

Would he fuck her after? Perhaps, but not necessarily. A punishment was not meant to end in a treat, but he might make an exception... Christ, she hoped so.

Naked, she dropped to her knees in front of him, head bowed and her hands resting palms up on her thighs. Tony said nothing, just rose from his chair and left the room. She heard him, first in her small kitchen, opening and shutting drawers, then his footsteps in her hallway heading back to her bedroom. She had no need to ponder what he might be doing. He was looking for an implement, something to spank her with. He would not be short of choices.

A couple of minutes later he returned. Her heart lurched, he had chosen well. Her silicon fish slice, light, supple, sure to deliver a burning sting if judiciously applied. And in his other hand, her small wooden cheeseboard, flat, smooth, heavy, a handle at one end. That would create a deep, solid whack, a slap that would sink deep into her flesh.

"I'll warm you up with my hand first, then move on to this." He flexed the fish slice between his hands before tossing it onto the low table beside the chair he had occupied previously. "Then, to make this a truly educative experience for you, I think this will serve us well. " He slapped the cheese board against his palm, causing a resounding crack to reverberate around the room. "I recalled how impressed you were with that paddle I bought for you a few weeks ago, but unfortunately I neglected to bring it with me today. This will deliver a similar sensation though."

Thea gasped. This was going to be severe. Tony meant business. Despite her trepidation though she was oddly calm. This felt right. It was as it should be. She had let her Dom down, briefly, but she had done it and there was a price to pay. She wanted to clean the slate now, and go forward.

"Do you have any questions? Or comments you'd like to offer?"

Thea shook her head. "No, Sir. I understand. I deserve to be punished. I just need you to forgive me, then I'll be able to forgive myself."

"I already forgive you, sweetheart. I love you, so how could I do otherwise? This is about teaching you who you are, what you are, and who you belong to." His tone had softened, warmed.

"I know it is. And, thank you, Sir."

The tender moment was over as quickly as it began. Tony was all business again, his stern Dom persona back, he exuded authority.

"Kneel on the chair." Tony tilted his chin at the seat he vacated earlier. "Face the back, fold your arms along the top and lean forward, your bottom lifted up as high as you can."

Thea got to her feet as gracefully as she was able given that her knees had turned to jelly. She climbed onto the chair, and adopted the position he required. She arched her back, lifting her buttocks for punishment.

"Do you have near neighbours who might be alarmed by the noise you're about to make?"

Thea nodded. "Yes, possibly. There's another flat on this floor, and I have neighbours above and below me."

"I thought so. A gag then." He stepped forward, pulling a pair of her sexiest stockings from his pocket. She last saw them in her bedroom drawer. "Open your mouth."

Thea obeyed, and Tony rolled one of the stockings into a ball and stuffed it in her mouth. He used the other to secure it in place, wrapping the length around her face and tying it at the back of her head.

"I don't intend to tie you up because you'll remain still. Won't you?"

Thea nodded, determined to accept what was coming without protest. She had earned this, and deserved whatever he might mete out.

"Your safe signal will be two sharp slaps on the back of the chair. If you use it, I'll stop. Your punishment will not be concluded though, and we'll return to it at a later time and continue until I'm satisfied you've learnt your lesson thoroughly. So, a hand spanking first then…" He moved to stand behind her. "Ready?"

Another nod, then Thea flinched as the first slap cracked across her right buttock. Tony was not going easy on her, even if this was only meant as a warm up. In seconds her backside was aflame, the rapid fire spanking covering every inch of her bottom and thighs. He continued to rain the sharp strokes across her tender skin until she was sobbing behind the gag, tears streaming unchecked down her face.

Tony didn't speak to her. He administered the punishment with ruthless, determined skill, heating her skin until she felt sure her backside must be glowing.

At last, he stopped. He rested his palm against her bottom, stroking to massage the pain away. Or drive it deeper. His other hand in the small of her back offered comfort, reassurance that this was done with love and caring, and that she would be safe.

He didn't hang about. Moments after he stopped spanking her with his hand he reached for the fish slice and the burning strokes started again. The implement made an ominous whooshing sound as he swung it, and with each whistling swipe through the air Thea clenched her bottom. She knew she should try not to, but couldn't help it.

"Surrender, and this will be over more quickly." His voice was cold, almost arctic.

Thea knew what he wanted, and that he would continue to punish her poor throbbing bottom until he was satisfied all resistance had gone. She concentrated on not tightening her muscles, working to accept all that he offered.

The blows all melted into one. Her bottom was on fire, her thighs too as he dropped stroke after sizzling stroke on her unprotected skin. She would inspect later, but knew her backside must be bright crimson. The pain was relentless, building, growing, spreading, consuming her. Thea sobbed, and screamed behind the gag, and was perversely comforted by its presence. She could let rip, scream her throat hoarse, with no danger of them being disturbed.

After what seemed an eternity Tony slowed the strokes, then stopped. He tossed the fish slice onto the seat beside her, and once again trailed his fingers over her abused buttocks.

Thea hissed, though she knew he wouldn't hear. He would know though, just as he always did.

"Your bottom's scorching. I think we're getting there. Just a little more, I think. To drive the message home."

Thea groaned to herself, but never contemplated slapping the back of the chair. Tony would decide when the punishment was finished, when she'd had enough, and only then would this be over. She would have gritted her teeth if the gag allowed that, but instead had to settle for biting down on the nylon stuffing her mouth.

She thought though that she might faint when he landed the first stroke with the heavy wood, and made a mental note to dump the vile cheeseboard in her bin first chance she got. It felt like the paddle be bought, but more. Much, much more. It was solid, weighty, each stroke catching the whole of her buttock. Tony put enough force behind the blows to send her jolting forward each time. She was beyond sobbing now, reduced to just grunting as each thunderous blow landed on her flaming backside. He had never hurt her like this before. His discipline had never been so sustained, nor so relentless. She knew he wasn't angry, not even a little, but he clearly meant to make this an experience she would never, ever forget.

He had succeeded. Thea's throat was hoarse, her screams now reduced to feeble whimpers. She lacked any strength to clench her bottom, nor even to hold her own weight any more. As she sagged and would have slumped onto the seat Tony slipped his arm under her stomach and held her up to receive the remaining strokes. Thea offered no resistance. She lay across his supporting arm like a rag doll as he continued to spank her.

"We're done." Thea was aware, dimly, of the thud as the makeshift paddle landed beside her knees on the seat. Her eyes were closed, she had no inclination to open them. She started to sink as Tony removed his arm.

"No, remain there. Don't move, and don't rub. You will stay in place, thinking about what just happened and why." His tone was implacable. Thea groaned, fearing that even now he might decide more punishment was required.

She dipped her head in silent acknowledgement of his command, and struggled to convince her muscles to cooperate. Her bottom and thighs were in agony, the pain excruciating but oddly cleansing too. Therapeutic. She had paid dearly for her error, but now the slate was clean.

Tony's footsteps crossed the room, and she heard the door click shut. She was bereft, wishing he hadn't left her on her own. She hated to be alone after a scene, even more so after a punishment. She needed to know he loved her, that they were all right. She wanted him to hold her, comfort her, make this go away.

Not the pain, she loved that, revelled in it, savoured the vicious burn as it caressed her heated skin, proof of her atonement. Physically she was fine, grounded. But her head was all over the place. Until her Master confirmed that she was still his, she was nothing. Nowhere.

"Tell me, Thea." His voice was low, and came from close by.

Not gone then? He hadn't left her alone. She should have known. Gentle hands were in her hair, untangling and untying the stocking which held her gag in place. It was gone, and the nylon in her mouth too. Her tongue was dry, but he held a bottle of water to her lips. She sucked, accepting his comfort, soaking it into her dry mouth as she absorbed his care into her needy, parched soul.

"What are you thinking? Right now, in this moment? Tell me."

"I love you."

"I love you too, sweet sub of mine."

"Yours. Yes. Please Sir, I need..."

"This?" He lifted her from the seat and slipped under her. He lowered her body on top of his, but turned her too so she was curled up in his lap.

"Yes Sir. This." Thea snuggled up, gripping the front of his shirt as he wrapped his arms around her. Then something else. Her duvet.

He must have brought that when he went to find the stockings. Always planning ahead, knowing what she would need. Always taking care of her. Suddenly she was sobbing again. "I'm sorry, so sorry."

"Sssh, I know. It's over. Done with. Cry if you need to, but stay still now. When you're ready to move I'll take you to bed. We'll talk more tomorrow, if you want to."

Bed? "Sir, will you fuck me?" She might enjoy that, though her arse was so sore she seriously wondered.

"No, not tonight though you do make one delectable little package with your bottom so gloriously punished. But I'm not going to fuck you, for two reasons. First, this was a punishment and I have no wish to dilute it. Nor to confuse it with anything else. When I spank you, seriously spank you as I just did, that isn't foreplay. And two, more than anything else right now, you need sleep. You've had a hell of a day."

He was right. Of course, as always, Tony knew. Smiling through her sobs, clinging to him as though her life depended on it, and right in that moment Thea wasn't at all sure it didn't, she relaxed in his arms. And fell asleep.

"No answer." Tony ended the call and slipped his phone back into his trouser pocket as he strolled back into Thea's bedroom. He carried a cup of steaming Earl Grey tea which he placed on the bedside table.

Still sleepy, Thea smiled at him and rolled onto her back in the bed. She winced as her tender buttocks pressed against the mattress, but the discomfort could not dim her contentment. For the first time in as long as she could remember, she felt whole. Grounded. She was the complete Thea Richmond and ready to face the world. Starting with this mysterious phone number.

Jerome had called back the previous evening to say that the surreptitious photographer in the dungeon had been ridiculously easy to bribe. He'd been paid two hundred pounds to take the picture, and would be more than happy to accept four hundred to provide details of his client. But there was a problem, he didn't know her name.

Both Tony and Thea did a double take at that, they had assumed their enemy would be male, though there was no particular reason for them to think so. All Jerome could tell them was that this woman had contacted their informant and told him she wanted compromising pictures of a specific couple at The Wicked Club, He'd had just few hours' notice. He was told to go to the club that same evening. He had their names, and a description, and his instructions were to wait for an opportunity to get a decent picture. Then he was to text the photo to a number he'd been given and the cash would be posted to him. His fee had arrived, ten crisp twenty pound notes in a brown envelope, so he assumed his client was satisfied with the bargain.

Jerome had extracted the contact number from him, the mobile phone that the picture had been texted to, and supplied that to Tony. He declared this the absolute best he could do and had virtually pleaded with Tony not to make a big fuss.

As she lay in bed, sipping her tea, Thea privately thought Jerome had got off lightly, The Wicked Club could have helped them to avoid all this if they'd been on the ball and confiscated that phone before the creep had a chance to send the picture to anyone. She had no confidence in the place any more and hoped Tony wouldn't insist on going back there. Ever.

The number was not one they recognised. Tony had dialled it immediately on the off chance that someone would answer and might give themselves away. So far they'd had no luck but Tony was right, they should keep trying. Later, back in her office, she would do what she could to trace it. If the phone was on a contract she might get somewhere. And in the meantime, they would have to hold their heads up and dare anyone to have a go. As Tony pointed out, there were some perks to being self-employed, and one of those was that no one could sack you.

He perched himself beside her on the bed. He looked to have been up for hours. "How are you this morning?"

"Good. I'm good. Really. And I'm sorry again about how I reacted yesterday."

"It's done. Finished. And you're better than good, baby. Did you sleep well?"
Thea smiled. He already knew the answer to that. He'd slept beside her.
"Yes, really well. Thank you for staying with me."
"My pleasure, sweetheart. But I'll need to be getting away soon. I need to pick up my stuff from home then go to the office. There's a lot to deal with today."
"I know that." She snuggled in closer as he draped an arm across her shoulders.
"I know you were meaning to be at Kershaw's today, but in the circumstances…"
"You're right. I'll come with you. We'll face them together. Do I have time for a shower?"
"Of course. I'll make more tea."

*****

Tony called a staff meeting, in the canteen. Thea reflected that this seemed to be becoming a habit of his. She stood at one end of the room as their employees filed in and seated themselves. Denise positioned herself on one side of her and Chris on the other. Both had been solid in their support when they had been summoned into Tony and Thea's office first thing, though in fairness they had had all night to discuss the bizarre picture each had found on their car as they left the previous evening. Eric too was on their side, and Thea knew he had been from the start. He had rushed to tell them as soon as he discovered the picture and had done what he could, belatedly, to contain the damage.
Isabel Barnard was still sulking. She had remained stony-faced during the meeting and offered no comment at all beyond acknowledging that she had been aware of the flyers distributed around the car park. If Tony had a view on her failure to alert him to it he did not allude to that.
He invited each manager to ask questions if they had any, or to make such comments as they found necessary. The only question came from Denise, who asked if Thea and Tony were in a

relationship. Tony responded that they were, that they had known each other for some time, and that their relationship was a serious one. Permanent, he hoped. Their colleagues expressed delight at that, and Eric went so far as to wonder if he should advise Mrs Henderson to buy a hat.

The shock factor was gone, everyone knew about the pictures, and beyond that their senior managers were of the opinion that the matter would soon be yesterday's news. The normally reserved Denise observed that the malicious bitch who had outed them might even have done them a favour, and the worst was already over. It was generally agreed that Tony was a popular figure at Dart, and Thea was becoming so. Most of their staff knew the part she'd played in getting Jeremy Malone reinstated. Dart employees were loyal, and pragmatic enough to appreciate a decent boss. How the company managers chose to spend their leisure time was of no concern to anyone else. Well, not much.

People were interested, some would be amused. Others might be jealous. But it would all blow over. Things always did.

Brazen it out. Chin up, and let Tony do most of the talking. That's what they'd agreed. And now came the moment of truth.

Tony had been seated at a table a few feet from her. The room fell silent when he got to his feet. Thea moved over to stand beside him. Tony smiled at her, then gazed across the hundred or so curious faces, all turned toward him.

He pulled a copy of the now infamous picture from his jacket pocket and held it up. "Has anyone not seen this?"

Silence.

"Does anyone here have any doubt that the two individuals in this picture are myself, and Mrs Richmond?"

More silence.

"Excellent. So we have that straight then. Just in case anyone is wondering, this picture was taken just under a week ago, at a club in the city. I hardly need to say, it was taken without our knowledge or permission. The club is a private venue, and we had every reason to suppose that anything taking place there was confidential. That confidence has been broken, and this is not a situation we can reverse."

He paused, but it was clear he had not finished. No one spoke. Tony swept his gaze across his attentive audience. "Before saying anything more I should explain something to you all, and this concerns consent. Those of us who choose to participate in the activities depicted in this image have consented to do so. It is our choice, and one we are free to make. Those who watch, those who observe, have also consented. You have not consented, you didn't choose to look at this picture. It was dumped on you whether you wanted it or not. To anyone here who finds themselves offended by what they have seen I can only apologise. You should not have been involved. But the fact is, each of you is involved, and you are now in possession of very private information, very personal information, about myself and Mrs Richmond. I hope you will treat this appropriately. I'm not about to insist you respect our confidentiality, you are under no such obligation. But I am entitled to require everyone who is employed at Dart Logistics to behave towards everyone else connected with this company with respect and courtesy. These rules apply equally, and encompass everyone. So, is there any person here who envisages any difficulty in complying with this?"

Still the room remained silent.

"Excellent. I appreciate though that for many it is difficult to speak out in a large group, especially about a sensitive issue such as this one. If anyone wishes to raise any concerns with me in private I am happy to hear them. Or you may prefer to talk to your head of department. So, that's all I need to say to you, but before we all get back to work, are there any further questions that I can deal with now?"

The silence was palpable. And uncomfortable. Thea cringed inwardly. Talk about an elephant in the room.

Tony shook his head. "You people are a disappointment to me. You've been shown a picture of your boss at a BDSM club, and no one has anything to say? Hell, if I was sitting where you are I'd have barrage of questions to ask."

There were a few nervous titters, a shuffling of feet, then a voice piped up from somewhere in the middle of the room. "Mr diMarco, what would you ask then? If you were us?"

Thea scanned the sea of faces in front of her but couldn't pick out who had spoken. Tony seemed to have no such difficulty.

"Well, Archie, I'd start by wanting to know where that club was and how much it would cost me to join. But that's just me and we all know now that I'm a kinky bastard."

There was collective gasp before the room erupted in laughter. And Thea knew it was going to be okay.

*****

"That went well." Thea perched her glasses on her nose as she opened up a spreadsheet on her PC. Her heart wasn't really in grappling with the complexities of their end of quarter projections, but her instincts were screaming at her to get back to normal. She shot a glance across the office to Tony, seated at the other desk. The door to Isabel's outer office stood open, but they knew she wasn't there. Isabel was taking her lunch down in the canteen. Thea was pondering how to broach the matter of the PA's continued service with Dart if her petulant mood continued. Tony had made it clear he was not about to put up with a negative attitude from anyone on his team, but even so Isabel had worked for him for several years. She was good at her job, or she had been. It was difficult to see how that would continue if the secretary refused to speak to either of them.

"Yeah. A little gallows humour goes a long way, I always think."

"It could have backfired. Referring to yourself as a kinky bastard…"

"I was banking on knowing my staff. They like a giggle, and you have to admit, this whole bloody mess has its comic side. BDSM always does." He cast a sardonic grin Thea's way. "Will you believe me if I tell you we'll look back on this in years to come, and laugh?"

"I'd have taken some convincing yesterday."

"And today?"

"Maybe. I confess the funny side of all this is a lot less obvious to me than it apparently is to you. Or to Archie Fellows."

Tony chuckled. "Ah yes, old Archie. He certainly opened the floodgates. I think you were right though, not to agree to incorporate flogging and nipple clamps in the revised disciplinary procedure."

Thea snorted. "I can't believe he actually said that. I didn't know where to look."

"You did fine. Really." He leaned forward, propping his elbows on the desk, his expression serious suddenly. "It was always going to be an ordeal, more so for you than me. We both knew that. Still, it's over now and you were brilliant. However uncomfortable, I'd rather they exhausted their curiosity all at once, and with us present. Far better that than to have everyone whispering in corners. It's out in the open now and I think our reputations will survive. Our staff may view both of us in a new light, but I feel we still have their respect. Don't you?"

"Mmm, time will tell. But yes, no one was overtly hostile. I'd have preferred to avoid all of this, but in the circumstances this is the best outcome we could have hoped for. And you're right. We had no choice. One thing still worries me though. What if whoever did this isn't done yet? What else might they be planning? And what was it all about anyway?"

"Who knows?" As he responded Tony picked up his phone and hit redial. He'd tried the mystery number several more times, always with no answer. Thea turned back to her screen.

They both heard it at the same time, a faint but distinct ringing. From somewhere close by. Thea's gaze snapped back to Tony. Their eyes met.

He ended the call and the ringing stopped. Coincidence?

"Try again," Thea whispered.

The ringing started up seconds after Tony finished dialling, and again it ceased when he hung up. The sound was coming from the outer office.

"Fucking hell." Tony got to his feet and strode out there. Thea was hard on his heels.

He dialled again, and they both stood transfixed as the trilling of a phone echoed around the otherwise silent space.

"The desk." Thea moved forward, examining Isabel's workspace for the telltale phone. "Nothing. But it's here somewhere."

"Keep looking. Underneath? In a drawer?"

Tony joined her and together they opened each drawer in turn. Thea crouched to peer under the desk, and spotted Isabel's bag tucked away there, out of sight. She dragged it out, and unzipped the top. The old fashioned Nokia lay on the top, its screen illuminated and 'unknown number' emblazoned across the display. Tony ended the call, the screen went dark and the trilling stopped. Thea stared at Tony, his expression of disbelief mirroring her own.

"Isabel? Isabel did this? But why?" Thea was incredulous.

"I intend to find out. First though, pass me that phone if you would." Thea obeyed, then straightened to stand beside Tony as he turned the phone on. He quickly located the pictures stored on it. There weren't many. A couple of shots of a house somewhere, several snaps taken at a wedding, and just one of her and Tony. That picture.

"I'll check her machine." Thea sat at Isabel's desk and fired up the PC there.

"What? Why?"

"She printed that off. She must have copied the file onto a computer, then sent it to the printer. My guess is she didn't do that at home."

"Right. She might have deleted it though."

"Maybe. If so, I'll get it back. I'm a forensic auditor, remember. If that picture is on this machine, or has ever been here, I'll find it."

Tony watched in silence as Thea spent the next several minutes checking through Isabel's recently altered files. She turned to him.

"It's here. Look."

She clicked the mouse to bring the image up on the screen. "The file has a number, but no name. It was created yesterday, and last accessed at eight minutes past four yesterday afternoon. I assume that's when she printed those flyers. Just before she left."

"Yes. Scattering them around the cars in our car park as she went."

"What's going on? What are you doing in here? That's my bag."

They turned. Isabel was framed in the open doorway, her half-finished cup of take-out Costa coffee in her hand. She looked furious.

"You have some explaining to do, Isabel." Tony didn't raise his voice. Neither did he respond to the implied criticism from his PA. Thea admired his restraint. She could not have summoned such control if her life depended on it. A Dom thing, no doubt.

"Me? What about you two? Searching through my private things. You had no right…"

"I do hope you're not about to start giving us a lecture on invasion of privacy, Isabel."

"I don't have to talk to you at all. Either of you."

"You do, if you want to carry on working here. I need a damn good explanation for this. And I need it now."

"Are you threatening to fire me?"

"Tony, we should—" Thea tried to interject, even in this situation her sense of procedure coming to the fore. Tony was having none of it.

"Yes. You've five minutes to convince me otherwise." His glare was implacable.

"So you're taking her side then?" Isabel spat the words at him. Her glance at Thea was laced with contempt.

"I am. Every time."

"You've only known her five minutes."

"What does that have to do with you? With any of this?"

"She swans in here as though she owns the place, telling us all the things we've been doing wrong. Who does she think she is? Jumped up cow."

"Isabel…" Thea couldn't miss the warning note in his growl, but evidently this was not a tone he used much with his PA as she seemed oblivious to it.

"You used to listen to me. You valued my advice. Not any more. Not since her ladyship arrived. It was bad enough that she got you to reinstate that lazy slob Malone, but when I walk in and find the pair of you all over each other in the office. Well, that's too much. She needed teaching a lesson."

"And you took it upon yourself to teach her? Is that how it was?"

"Someone had to."

"So let me make sure I'm getting this. In order to 'teach her a lesson' you paid someone to follow Thea and me to a club, and take a compromising picture of us. Then you printed that picture and handed it out to everyone who works here. You even went over to the home of Thea's other employer and treated him to a copy too."

"I thought he should know what sort of a person he had working for him."

"He knows what sort of person Thea is. So do I. So does everyone else here. She's a consummate professional, brilliant at her job. Dart was lucky to get her. Kershaw's too."

"She's a slag."

There was a brief pause, then. "And you're out of work. Leave now, Isabel."

"I'm going nowhere."

"Out. Now. Under your own steam, or with the help of security." He picked up her bag and handed it to her.

"My phone?"

"Ah, right." Tony still had it in his hand and turned it on. He navigated back to the picture and deleted it.

"You had no right to do that. That's interfering with my property."

"Just get out, Isabel. If you're still in this room by the time I count to five, I'll have security remove you from the premises."

"You can't just fire me. I have rights."

"Two."

"I'll have you in front of a tribunal. I'll—"

"Three."

He nodded at Thea, which she took to be a signal to contact security. She picked up the phone on Isabel's desk and dialled zero. Isabel remained rooted to the spot, her expression belligerent.

"Four."

"Hello, Security? Could you send someone up to Mr diMarco's office please? Immediately. Thank you." Thea replaced the handset and turned to face her adversary again. Or she would have. Isabel was already scuttling out of the door, her bag clutched to her chest. Tony strolled to the window. "If she's not crossing the car park in twenty seconds I'll have her found and ejected from the building." Thea went to stand next to him. They waited in silence, Thea counting in her head. She reached eighteen before the outer door opened, and together they watched Isabel Barnard hurtle from the front entrance and dash down the half dozen or so steps. She headed to her car and within a few seconds was roaring out of the gate.

"Will we see her again?"

"I sincerely hope not."

"I can't believe she was so jealous. Resentful. Of me. Is that what all this was about? Just that?"

"It seems like it."

"I thought she liked me. We got on fine. Well, we did at first…" Thea was bemused suddenly, now that the crisis seemed to be over. Baffled at the bizarre attitude taken by the other woman. Talk about disproportionate.

"I had that impression too. She certainly seemed to like me. I'd thought we were close. Still… we now know who, and we know why up to a point though I agree with you, it all seems a bit off the wall. But we don't know how."

"What do you mean?"

"How did she know we'd be at the club that night? Shit, I didn't even know myself until that same afternoon."

"Me neither. You told me after the managers' meeting that afternoon. When we both stayed back in the conference room. No one else knew but us two."

"So…"

Thea stood suddenly. "I have an idea. Where's that guy from security?"

As though summoned by Thea's words the man arrived at the entrance to the office suite. "Is there a problem here? You called security."

"Yes. I need to look at some CCTV recordings. The corridor outside the conference room to be specific."

"I see, miss. Is there any particular date you're interested in?"

"Last Wednesday afternoon. Around three."

Thirty minutes later Thea and Tony huddled around her computer viewing the security images which had been sent up from their archives.

"So you were right. Isabel hung around outside after everyone else left. She was eavesdropping."

"Yes, it seems so." Thea was pleased to have found the remaining part of the jigsaw, though she took little satisfaction from any of it. "But why?"

"Curiosity perhaps. I suppose it's fair to say that by this time she didn't trust us. Either of us. She must have heard you mention The

Wicked Club, and assuming she heard the rest of our conversation she'd have been able to work out what sort of place it was. My hunch is that the picture was a spur of the moment thing. Maybe she didn't actually intend to use it. But then we had that row a couple of days later, when she walked in on us in here. And she was so angry about Jeremy Malone. Maybe she just acted on the spur of the moment, out of temper."

"Maybe. I guess we'll never know. One thing I do know though."

"What's that?"

"I need a new PA. Can you recommend anyone?"

"Leave it with me." Thea closed down the CCTV link and turned to face Tony again. "Sir?"

"Yes, Thea?"

"Do you think we've earned half a day off?"

"What do you have in mind? A spot of shopping perhaps? Maybe we could take in a film."

"I thought we might just go home."

"Home, Mrs Richmond." He glanced at his watch. "It's not two o'clock yet. On a weekday too."

"I know that, Sir."

"Are you angling for another spanking, Thea?"

"I am, Sir."

"I could oblige you here. It would be no trouble."

"I'd prefer to go home. If you don't mind, Sir. We can be more—unrestrained there."

"Unrestrained? Tell me, Thea—exactly who are you, and what have you done with Mrs Richmond? She would never have countenanced sneaking off for a spanking and a spot of unrestrained fucking on a Tuesday afternoon."

Thea got to her feet with a smile and moved across the room to Tony's desk, unbuttoning the top three buttons of her navy blue silk shirt as she went. She leaned over to whisper in his ear, ensuring he had an unimpeded view of her lace-adorned cleavage. "Mrs Richmond is a fine manager. I'm sure we both have the utmost respect for her. It's true that she doesn't do unrestrained very well but she's working on it. And she's a fast learner, Sir." She kissed his neck. "Home?"

Tony grabbed his jacket from the back of his chair. "I'll drive."

About the Author

USA Today best-selling author Ashe Barker has been an avid reader of fiction for many years, erotic and other genres. She still loves reading, the hotter the better. But now she has a good excuse for her guilty pleasure – research.

Ashe tends to draw on her own experience to lend colour, detail and realism to her plots and characters. An incident here, a chance remark there, a bizarre event or quirky character, any of these can spark a story idea.

Ashe lives in the North of England, on the edge of the Brontë moors and enjoys the occasional flirtation with pole dancing and drinking Earl Grey tea. When not writing – which is not very often these days - her time is divided between her role as taxi driver for her teenage daughter, and caring for a menagerie of dogs, tortoises. And a very grumpy cockatiel.

At the last count Ashe had around forty titles on general release with publishers on both sides of the Atlantic, and several more in the pipeline. She writes M/f, M/M, and occasionally rings the changes with a little M/M/f. Ashe's books invariably feature BDSM. She writes explicit stories, always hot, but offering far more than just sizzling sex. Ashe likes to read about complex characters, and to lose herself in compelling plots, so that's what she writes too.

Ashe has a pile of story ideas still to work through, and keeps thinking of new ones at the most unlikely moments, so you can expect to see a lot more from her.

Ashe loves to hear from readers. You can email her direct on ashe.barker1@gmail.com

Also by Ashe Barker

Resurrection

The past is only a heartbeat away

Right from the start she knew it wasn't about love.

As the youngest daughter of a wealthy family in medieval England, Lady Jane of Acton has been betrothed to Ged Twyfford, the son of the Earl of Roseworth, since she was a baby. A dynastic marriage such as theirs is about power and property, not love but even so Jane desperately yearns for her husband's approval. But Ged's rare visits to her bed are for the sole purpose of producing an heir, and she's even failed at that. How can Jane win her husband over when she cannot even be the wife he needs her to be?

Would one last chance be enough? Could he make things right, even now?

Ged Twyfford doesn't know what he's missing in life. A powerful vampire, he's lived for close to six hundred years and seen a lot during his time but his past still haunts him. On a whim, he purchases Roseworth castle, the keep he used to rule as lord. Mostly in ruins now, the castle is a shell of what it was when he was still a mortal but Ged is determined to make Roseworth his home again. Maybe this is what he's been missing, maybe he needs a place to belong at last.

When a woman emerges from the lake beside his castle, looking and sounding a lot like the wife he lost over five centuries ago, Ged assumes she's a witch out to dupe him. But what if she *is* who she claims to be? Ged finally realizes just what he had, and just how precious to him was the wife he betrayed all those hundreds of years ago.

Do they have a second chance or is it just too late to start over?

First Impressions

First Impressions can be deceptive.

Aidan Blake needs a plumber. Fast. His boiler is dead, his creaky old house crumbling around him. When his elderly neighbour recommends a local trader, George Mahon, Aidan jumps at the prospect of hot water and warm radiators.

But George, short for Georgina, is not exactly what he had in mind. He was expecting
something else entirely. A man for one thing, not the gorgeous single mother he finds in his house at the end of a long day of work.

Aidan turns out to be full of surprises too. Who would have imagined the smartly dressed businessman would have a BDSM playroom in his attic and a collection of whips and canes that makes George's head spin. And her bottom clench, though that's another matter entirely. What does a girl have to do to get to play with those toys?

Just ask, it would seem. As they enter into a professional and personal agreement which soon blossoms into a sultry, kinky relationship, George continues to be surprised by Aidan's kindness and generosity, not to mention his skill with a spanking paddle.

First impressions aside, the two begin to build something together. And while they peel back the layers to discover their hidden depths, the old house yields up the mysteries of its own secret past. They soon realise that at first glance, nothing is ever quite as it seems.

Shared by the Highlanders

After she becomes lost in a thick mist while hiking near the borders of Scotland, Charlene Kelly is shocked to encounter two men on horseback. To her horror, the pair—both of whom are dressed in Scottish tartans—accost her and won't let her go. Though the men speak with accents so strong they seem to come from another era, Charlene is able to gather that they believe she is a thieving boy. Unsure what else to do, Charlene plays along.

When Will Sinclair and Robbie MacBride discover that their captive is in fact a woman—and quite a beautiful one at that—there is only one thing to be done. She must be punished for her deception, and punished thoroughly. A switch applied to her bare bottom does the job well, and soon enough the two men are comforting Charlene as she nurses her bright red, sore backside.

Upon learning that the highlanders are hand-carrying an important message from Elizabeth of England to the court of Mary, Queen of Scots, it finally dawns on Charlene that she is no longer in her own time. Though she is desperate to find a way home, Will and Robbie are both unlike any man she has ever met, and their unabashed dominance awakens in her a powerful need to submit. Soon enough, she finds herself blushing with shame and quivering with desire as she is taken long and hard by two rugged highlanders at once. But can these hardened warriors keep her safe from the perils of a world far more dangerous than the one she left behind?